D1603116

*W*hat the critics are saying...

ɕↄ

"In the year 2015, a breed of super soldiers has been created. Some of them wish to emulate Hitler and create the perfect race, while others become Black Knights, guardians of normal humans. The ending leaves you longing to learn more about these warriors and the world they try to defend." ~ *Romantic Times*

"I have been much anticipating the second book in the Underground Guardians series as I've been interested in seeing more of the characters introduced in PROTECTOR, Diego in particular. Lisa Renee Jones does not disappoint with HEALER" ~ *Romance Junkies.*

"Awesome book! Renee Jones has done a wonderful job creating a plot that has twists and turns enough to keep readers on the edge of their seats" ~ *The Romance Studio*

"Underground Guardians: Healer by Lisa Renee Jones is one of those things like chocolate—something that makes life worth living. One great book in a series is a fluke; two is a definite sign of delicious things to come from a talented author. Now that I am hooked, I hope Ms.

Jones intends to continue writing about her Black Knights until we beg her to stop!" ~ *EcataRomance Reviews*

HEALER

UNDERGROUND GUARDIANS

LISA RENEE JONES

ELLORA'S CAVE
ROMANTICA PUBLISHING

An Ellora's Cave Romantica Publication

www.ellorascave.com

Healer

ISBN #1419953516
ALL RIGHTS RESERVED.
Healer Copyright © 2005 Lisa Renee Jones
Edited by Pamela Cohen
Cover art by Syneca

Electronic book Publication July 2005
Trade paperback Publication May 2006

Excerpt from *Red Hot Secrets* Copyright © Lisa Renee Jones, 2005

Warning:

The following material contains graphic sexual content meant for mature readers. This story has been rated S (S-ensuous) by a minimum of three independent reviewers.

Ellora's Cave Publishing offers three levels of Romantica™ reading entertainment: S (S-ensuous), E (E-rotic), and X (X-treme).

S-*ensuous* love scenes are explicit and leave nothing to the imagination.

E-*rotic* love scenes are explicit, leave nothing to the imagination, and are high in volume per the overall word count. In addition, some E-rated titles might contain fantasy material that some readers find objectionable, such as bondage, submission, same sex encounters, forced seductions, and so forth. E-rated titles are the most graphic titles we carry; it is common, for instance, for an author to use words such as "fucking", "cock", "pussy", and such within their work of literature.

X-*treme* titles differ from E-rated titles only in plot premise and storyline execution. Unlike E-rated titles, stories designated with the letter X tend to contain controversial subject matter not for the faint of heart.

*A*lso by Lisa Renee Jones

ဆာ

Addicted
Christmas King
Hurt So Good
Red Hot Secrets
Underground Guardians: Protector

*A*bout the *A*uthor

ဆာ

Lisa Renee Jones lives in Austin, Texas. She owned and operated a seven-office staffing company for eleven years. She discovered a love for writing in 2003 and sold her business, and now has a dozen published titles.

Lisa welcomes mail from readers. You can write to her c/o Ellora's Cave Publishing at 1056 Home Avenue Akron OH 44310-3502.

Healer

Underground Guardians

ဢ

Prologue I

ᏸᎧ

The world will never be the same.

In the year 2015, Area 51 proved to be more than a place where alien rumors existed. It was here that the United States government decided to create Super Soldiers. Alien DNA purporting to be immunizations was injected into elite soldiers and a new race was created— soldiers with unique powers. Humans to the normal eye, but not quite so human anymore. Some stronger and more powerful than others, but all dangerous. All were fighters with incredible strength and speed along with unique mind powers. Some have fangs and claws they can use at will. Rapid metabolism has given them an amazing ability to heal from injuries. With muscles like steel, a simple bullet is no longer deadly.

They are deadly fighting machines.

Along with this new breed of soldier came a thirst for power. A thirst he intended to sate. This soldier developed a vision for a "perfect race". David Alexander became the new Hitler, even calling his followers, enhanced soldiers, the 'Arions', as Hitler had his perfect race.

The first step in his plan to rule humanity was to take over Area 51. His one obstacle is breeding and he has a team of scientists working to ensure it is conquered. An Arion can only bear children if mated. An Arion only has one true mate. This means he must find compatible women for his men. A task he finds difficult. This leaves him looking for genetic and alternative birthing methods.

He uses humans like tokens, promising them power or conversion, or threatening their families.

Once he perfects a way to grow his race, there will be no stopping him.

But there is one other challenge David must overcome to achieve world dominance. Mason Alexander, his brother, has risen as a leader and Guardian of the humans. David wants Mason to join him, and they will be stronger. Two brothers ruling the world.

Mason will never go to the dark side. He and many other Super Soldiers will do whatever it takes to stop the Arions.

Because good *must* conquer evil.

Prologue II
Nevada, 2016

ഔ

Diego Montez stepped outside of the cave, feeling the fresh air like a long-lost friend. Living his life beneath the ground, in the secret society of his people, he sometimes forgot how amazing the world above could be. It had been over a year since life had changed so drastically. Since that day in the lab when a government experiment to mix alien DNA with a human's had backfired.

Sometimes he still felt like he was living some bad dream. Elite soldiers, he included, had been told they were being immunized. Instead, they were turned into a new race. But the government's deceit became their demise. One power-hungry soldier developed aspirations of ruling a better race. He'd overtaken the research facility and declared war against humanity. Following in Hitler's footsteps, he named his people Arions...the perfect race.

And somehow, amongst the darkness of the events, he'd found himself claimed by the Arions.

But just as he knew the difference between right and wrong, good and evil always managed to split from one another. Diego knew if he waited, his opportunity to fight for the right side would come. And he'd been right. Soon the war became about two brothers, one an honorable leader and the other a power-hungry dominator. A silent war for total control now raged hidden from humanity. Diego thought back to his early days, trapped with the evil half of the two men.

It had been pure hell.

Now a part of the Black Knights, the good part of this craziness, he was both doctor and warrior. One with the challenge of learning the healing ways of a new race. The challenges had been immense. Gifted with special mind powers, the Knights had not learned to master them, as had their enemy. They needed help.

Marcella Hunter, a woman considered more myth than reality, might just be the answer. Said to heal with her touch and move objects with her mind, many called her the devil. Some, a saint.

And now, as he slid onto a motorcycle and kickstarted it into action, Diego prepared himself for his newest challenge. He was going to his homeland. Mexico. To Monterey, the city of his birth, and there he would find Marcella Hunter before the enemy did.

Chapter One

🔊

Everything male in him roared to life the moment he saw Marcella Hunter.

With one booted foot crossed over the top of the other, leaning against the hotel's exterior brick wall, Diego Montez appeared relaxed. He'd had plenty of practice maintaining a cool facade. Calm and unflappable under pressure, he was a doctor, a healer for his people, who knew how to take things with ease while others panicked. Despite his exterior, a combination of arousal and possessiveness lurked beneath his surface, growing with each passing second. It burned within his veins like hot lava. Even as he grasped for control of his unexpected reaction, Marcella Hunter walked towards him with a sexy little sway to her curvy yet slim hips. She was a seduction by pure existence, evoking feelings both hot and protective. Unfamiliar feelings consuming both body and mind. He forgot all else.

Forgot his mission.

Petite, with long, auburn hair that fell in little ringlets around her heart-shaped face, she was perfection from head to toe. A flowing skirt caught in the wind, hugging her lush body and displaying curves in all the right places. She dressed simply with no flair, no desire to stand out.

But there was nothing simple about this woman.

His body responded even before his mind. His cock hardened and his pulse pounded triple time. He was aroused for the first time in well over a year—since he became what he called "GTECH" enhanced—in other words he had been genetically upgraded using alien DNA. The kick of passion he felt was like a white-hot rush and a complete shock. He no longer had the ability to feel this way for just any female. There was only one he could desire…his mate.

Why, he didn't know. It was a mystery he continued to work on unraveling. They'd only discovered it had something to do with a certain human genetic line. And only when properly mated could reproduction occur. His enemy hunted those within this group of females with vengeance, determined to grow their new race.

To find his own partner in this new assignment was an unexpected twist to his already complicated position.

She moved towards the Monterey Hightower Hotel, two people beside her. One, an older, Hispanic grandmotherly type. The other was a thirty-something male, also Hispanic, with military-style dark hair. Diego instantly disliked the man. He didn't like the way he seemed to hover near Marcella as if she was his captive. Nor did he like the possessive way he touched her elbow.

An animalistic urge to claim her as his own roared to life, screaming at his body, mind and soul—begging for action. Shackling the turbulence of his feelings, he forced out a slow breath. Drawing unneeded attention could be dangerous. His enemy, the Arions, had become sneaky, using humans to do their bidding. They lured them with the promise of money and power and even special powers.

Control was everything.

And he'd always considered himself a man of control, but as the man beside Marcella ran his hand down her arm, Diego all but came unglued. At that moment, he wondered if he was losing grip on that aspect of his personality. Discarding the idea, he reminded himself of the facts as he knew them. His genetic enhancements didn't change who he was as a person.

It gave him special talents, more physical power and a multitude of other things. The man, good or evil, remained the same. But it didn't change the fact that these enhancements had used Area 51 discoveries. He was no longer human. Another life form had become a part of his genetic code. A new race existed. One that was far more aggressive than humans. They were hunters who fought for what they wanted, driven by more animal instinct than human motives.

Even he, as a doctor, a man who had lived his life to care for others, sometimes felt his beast rise to life.

Without taking his eyes off the woman he would soon call his own, he turned up his enhanced senses to scan for danger. At the same time, as if she sensed his presence, Marcella's eyes moved to his. Her steps slowed. For long seconds, it was as if time stopped. As if their souls were merging.

Suddenly, she was walking in his direction.

* * * * *

Marcella needed to know who he was.

She approached the dark, sexy stranger, feeling a sense of urgency she didn't quite understand. God, he was big. The dark t-shirt he wore clung to rippling muscles—defined and perfectly developed—but without bulk. Tall, broad and with short hair, he was hard to miss. Even more so for her because somehow, she knew him. She just didn't know how. What she felt was very…intimate. Sensual.

"Marcella, come back here."

The voice of her bodyguard, David Martinez, registered but was ignored. She was in no danger from this man. She felt below his surface. Knew him to be no risk. Knew him beyond what she should. He didn't move as she approached. But he watched her every step.

She stopped directly in front of him. "Do I know you?"

"No," he said, his voice low and sultry with just a tiny hint of amusement in it. "Not yet."

Marcella shoved a lock of hair behind her ear. "Who are you?"

A deep voice called her from behind. "Marcella." David was now standing directly behind her. "Come with me," he said. It was a command.

"She stays," Diego said, his voice just tight enough to hint at anger he couldn't quite contain.

Marcella turned to David, cutting off the words he was about to speak. "Give me a minute."

David didn't waver from his position. "Marcella—"

"No. Give me a minute." This time she spoke with authority, clearly making it known she was in charge, not him.

David looked at Diego, their eyes locking in a challenge. Marcella didn't miss the undertone of battle between them. Great. Just what she needed, some kind of macho showdown.

"David, please," she said with a plea in her voice. "I know him. Give me a minute."

David looked as if he might argue, his eyes searching her face before he finally turned and walked towards the other woman.

"Who is he to you?" Diego asked.

She turned to face him. "How is that your business?"

One brow inched upward in challenge, an undertone of interest in both his voice and words. "Everything about you is my business, and you know it. Already you have admitted knowing me." He paused. "Because you do."

His words should have offended. Instead, they aroused. She wanted this man. It was frightening how much. Her head tilted to the side as she studied his handsome features. She did know him, but perhaps on a level no one but she could understand. But then, maybe that wasn't true. This man was different. He felt what she did. She could see it in his sultry, midnight eyes.

Feeling a bit nervous because of the impact he was having on her, it took effort to find her voice. "You said I didn't know you. Not yet, but I do. How?"

"In time you will understand." He held her gaze as he spoke the silky words. His voice, deep and sexy, seemed laced with a caress. Her skin felt the warmth of a touch. Her stomach fluttered. "Right now we must leave. You are in danger."

She laughed. Nervous. "Right. Leave. With you? You have to be joking." His scent traveled the warm air, lacing her nostrils with its addictive male allure and taking the edge off her words.

His reply was firm, full of resolve. "I couldn't be more serious."

His eye held hers. It was as if he invited her to look deep into his soul. To confirm the intent in his words. But

17

she couldn't focus on anything except the simmering sensuality just below his surface. It had been many years since she had felt the heat of physical need. Her gifts had given her a duty to help those in need. Her own satisfaction had never been her quest. So why now was this dark stranger making her feel such awareness? Such attraction? Every nerve ending she owned had gone from dormant to wildly alive.

A sudden shiver raced up her spine. "Who are you?"

"Who I am is not as important as why I'm here. As I said, you're in grave danger. Your abilities are a resource some would abuse."

Obviously, he knew things about her a mere stranger wouldn't. Or shouldn't. "How would you know?"

"Does it matter?" he asked

"Maybe you're the danger."

"Your enemy is mine as well. And you know those things which make you unique are gifts but they also put you at risk."

"If I have gifts, and I'm not saying I do, how can I be sure you aren't after them?" She crossed her arms in front of her body.

"You know I'm not." He said his words with absolute certainty.

She stared at him. It was true. She did know. Still... "This is crazy."

He held out his hand, and there was expectancy to the action. For her to simply accept his words. For her to trust him. "We must leave," Diego said. "The people who hunt you are like none you have ever known. You will not resist them without my help."

His words made her insides quiver because deep down she did believe him. There was no logic to why. But then, her mind knew things others had to reason to conclude. For Marcella, things simply were or they weren't. Someone was hunting her. She'd felt it for a lifetime, but over the course of the last few days, there had been something darker in the shadows. A force so evil it had tainted the very air she breathed. But going out in public made her so nervous she decided not to overreact. She didn't want to upset her aunt over a bad case of apprehension. Though Marcella barely remembered the loss of her parents, it was still a source of pain to her aunt. But the feeling hadn't gotten better. It seemed to be growing.

Even being on edge, when she'd seen Diego watching her, she'd been certain he wasn't the source of her discomfort. Still was.

His hand stayed mid-air, palm up in invitation. She looked down at it. Large but somehow gentle, it welcomed her. His soul was compassionate. But there was also a warrior in him, deadly and intent on winning. He would fight to death if needed. And the color of his skin, a milk chocolate tone, was a contrast to her pale, white skin. An image of them naked, dark and light entwined, came from nowhere and made her eyes dart to his.

"I can't leave," she insisted. "No. I'm not going anywhere with you."

"Yes," he said, no give to his voice. "You are."

Marcella couldn't believe she was even having this conversation. "No. I have a bodyguard." Her eyes went to David and then back to Diego. "He takes good care of me." She hoped she sounded convincing. Diego seemed so sure of himself. She was a bit concerned he might just grab her and go. Even sensed he considered as much.

Yet calling for David seemed the wrong choice.

Diego's eyes darted behind her towards David. "So he's your bodyguard."

He studied him and then looked back at her. "He wants to fuck you." His eyes held anger and his tone a hint of hostility.

Marcella gasped, shocked at the abruptness of his words. Most people didn't verbalize such thoughts. "He does not!" She was quite certain Diego was a kind and gentle man. Why she didn't know but it was there, a part of him. She always got a sense about a person. With Diego it was clearer than normal but at the same time unlike anything she'd read from another. There was something she didn't understand. It conflicted with the other things she sensed. It was…more animalistic beneath his surface.

His look was a reprimand. "You know I speak the truth. You sense what he feels for you even if you choose to pretend it's something different. Some form of affection not built of lust." He paused. "Besides, he is not capable of protecting you as I am."

She frowned at his arrogance. "He is just as good as you." But she knew he wasn't.

"No." His lips twitched as if he knew she had lied. "He cannot win against the enemy that hunts you."

She didn't like the way he phrased things. It rang so true to her feelings over the past days, it was frightening. "Do you have to use the word *hunt*?" It bothered her. Maybe because it was so true to the dark feelings she had been having. "For all I know, you are the one hunting me. Perhaps you are simply trying to confuse me."

"We both know you can sense my motives. I speak the truth. Nothing less. Nothing more. I am your only hope of survival. You must come with me."

"I'm staying," she responded instantly and then added, "I'm here to heal a child. I will not walk away from her need." Why she felt the need to justify declining to go with him, she didn't know. This man was a stranger.

He took a long time to answer. "When do you see the child?"

Why she told him anything, she didn't know. Something inside her wanted to trust him. And she had been conditioned to let no one into her inner circle. It could get her killed or captured like some animal. "Soon. Tonight. In just a few hours."

His eyes narrowed and she had the distinct feeling he reached for her mind. A whisper of a touch, but it was there. "We leave the instant you have completed your duty."

"Duty?" she asked. "Why did you call it that?"

"Because that is how you see it." There was absoluteness to his words.

He had touched her mind as she had thought. But it had been done with such precision even with her level of skill he had been barely perceivable. "How would you know that?"

Taking her off guard, he pushed off the wall, closing the distance between them. He stood within a breath of touching her. The heat he generated warmed her skin, stirring a flutter in her stomach.

"What are you doing?" she demanded, but the words were barely there.

His body was big enough to frame hers, and again, unbidden images flashed in her mind. Him naked. Her naked. Him on top of her, inside her, all around her.

He lowered his head near her ear, his breath trickling along her neck, enticing goose bumps along her skin. "I know you, as you do me." Her mind processed his words, even as her body responded to the deep tone of his voice as if it were a physical caress. Her nipples tingled. Her thighs ached. "I can feel you," he said," as you do me."

She swallowed and raised her eyes to his. "Who are you?"

"Meet me in this exact spot at midnight. If you don't, I'll come for you."

Who did he think he was? He couldn't just order her around. "I won't be here."

His gaze locked with hers, and she heard his voice in her head. *You will.*

Her eyes went wide. She'd never met anyone who could communicate with her telepathically. "Who are you?"

He ignored her question. "Go take care of the child. We don't have much time."

And then his hand slid to the side of her face. The touch was like an electric charge. It, no, *he* ran though her body, touching each and every nerve ending. Her nipples tightened, her heart kicked up a beat and she had to fight the urge to reach up and touch his hand. She needed to touch him as he did her. Speaking didn't even seem an option. For the briefest of moments, she was completely lost in this man.

"Marcella!"

David's voice, bellowing through the air, snapped her back into reality. She forced herself to step away from his touch. And it took effort. Lots of it. "I have to go."

"Meet me or I will come for you."

Chapter Two

🆂

Walking through the lobby of the hotel, Marcella's mind replayed her encounter with Diego. The elegance of the white and black tiled floors and matching furnishings were a shadow in her mind. The man she had just met consumed her thoughts. She could still smell the spicy sweetness of his cologne. And God, how she felt that one simple touch. Dampness clung to her panties, making her all too aware of her extreme reaction to a mere stranger. Plain and simple, she wanted him.

A stranger.

It was the craziest thing she had ever experienced. Her mind raced as she tried to comprehend not only what she felt for him but also why he was so familiar. Not only that, he'd spoken of danger. It seemed she needed to talk to David and her aunt. But she hesitated and she wasn't sure why. She needed peace and quiet to focus. The answers would come if she concentrated fully. An impossible task in a crowded lobby. And then, of course, there was David to deal with. He simmered with agitation. Even distracted by thoughts of Diego, she could feel his mood.

The more she was around someone, the more sensitive she became to their emotions. For the most part, she knew how to block things and only see or hear them when she wanted to. Some people, David included, were so intense, they were hard to ignore. He tended to be a bit testy when he didn't get his way.

He'd get over it. He always did.

She was just about to step into the check-in line when David's hand settled on her arm. Reacting, she turned to him, a question in her expression.

His face held a scowl. "You hired me to be your bodyguard." There was a bite to his voice. "If I'm to protect you, you have to listen to me."

She didn't like his sharp tone. Wanting his way was one thing. Expressing it rudely was another. Marcella was a quiet person. She'd been sheltered and hidden from much of the world. But she also had a strong aunt who had taught her to stand up for her beliefs. She heard of her mother's bravery. Those stories pressed Marcella to help the needy despite the risk. And they pushed her aunt to ease her protectiveness enough to support Marcella's efforts.

"Aren't you going to respond?" he asked, impatience in his tone.

She stiffened. "I was giving you a minute to retract your bossy words. Since you didn't, I will remind you I *hired* you to ensure my safety, not baby-sit me."

David didn't seem fazed. "Who was that man?" he demanded, lips thin.

The same thing Diego had asked about him. Each man wanted to know about the other. "Why do you care?" she countered, her eyes searching his. Had Diego been right? Did David want her? Was he jealous? Her stomach lurched as the answer came to her. Yes, David did indeed want her. Which made life much more complicated than it needed to be. She had too much to worry about as it was. Like a child who needed saving. Perhaps she had always known David wanted her. It was one of those things she simply preferred to dismiss. Maybe because if it existed, it had been carefully checked. Therefore, it was not an attention grabber. Until now.

"Answer the question," he said, using a sharp tone so very unlike the low monotone he typically addressed her with. It made her do a double take.

She had no intention of explaining what was going on with Diego. David would freak. "I told you I know him."

His eyes flickered with something she couldn't quite identify, and her mind was too consumed to focus beyond the obvious. David was an attractive man. Hispanic with blue eyes, he was quite striking. Most women found him appealing. But she wasn't 'most women'. She didn't respond to the physical side of life. Or so she had thought. Diego had changed things. That, in and of itself, was enough to make her nervous. Why did she respond with such vibrant physical and emotional completeness to him?

"How?"

She stiffened, realizing she had slipped into her own thoughts. Refocusing, she met David's probing stare. She felt uptight under his scrutiny, not sure what she wanted to tell him. Lies were not her forte. She liked honesty. "I told you I know him. That should be enough." And she did. Somehow. Some way. She knew him.

He paused a bit too long, as if he was trying to decide if he believed her. "But can you trust him?" he said, teeth clenched.

Suddenly she realized her aunt had disappeared. "Where's Catherine?" she asked, starting to turn away from him.

"She's sitting down. Her feet hurt."

Marcella bit her bottom lip. "I told her she shouldn't have come. I worry about her." Marcella barely remembered her mother. Her aunt had raised her since she was a small child. Her mother's powers had made her entire family victims to power-hungry monsters. And one night years before, her father had died protecting her mother. Then her mother had taken her own life rather than allow herself to become an experiment.

In turn, Marcella had lost her forever.

David's voice held impatience as he directed the conversation back to Diego. "Now answer my question. How do you know you can trust this man?"

She gave her head a slight shake, pulling herself back to the present. The past was a dark place to visit. But then, now, this moment, David wasn't all so bright and cheery himself. He was jealous. She hated to admit it, but now that she had opened her eyes and mind to the obvious, she saw it. Guilt made her frustration ease. Never in a million years would she taunt him.

Reaching out, she touched his shoulder. "He means me no harm." At least she hoped. He didn't feel dangerous. Still, he had powers. The possibility he might have the ability to shield her from his true intent had to be considered. "Thank you for worrying but let's focus on why we're here. There's a little girl who needs me." And to Marcella that was what ranked number one. She was a Healer, given a gift. The same one her mother and father died to ensure wasn't abused. And she would do the same if ever needed. "Please make contact. The sooner I see her, the better."

After several seconds, his expression softened. That was enough for her. Turning away from him, she didn't wait for a reply. He was calming down now. All she wanted to do was check into the hotel and take care of business. Okay, so that wasn't entirely true. She needed alone time to think. About how serious the danger she was in might be. Was it enough to upset her aunt? And about her stranger. About Diego. For some reason she wanted to use his name. It felt familiar and right. Diego...

Just thinking of him made her heart kick up a beat.

She stepped into line, hoping David would do as she'd said. Her back to him, she counted to three. When he didn't say or do anything, she let out a breath. At least for the moment, David was done pressing. How could she explain what was going on when she didn't understand herself? In the year David had been with her, his ability to keep her hidden had been perfection. Yet...Diego had found her. And the danger he spoke of...why did David not know about it?

But she had known. She'd just dismissed it as nerves. Uneasiness began to build as she tuned into the feeling she had been having, this time seizing it rather than discarding it. By the time she was holding her room key in her hand, she was quite certain Diego was right. She was in danger. And it wasn't from him. The darkness she felt was sinister. Diego was not.

Ready to get to her room, Marcella went in search of her aunt, glad David had yet to return. She needed some time to decide what she should or shouldn't tell him. After all, he *was* her bodyguard. Surely, he should be told there was imminent danger.

In an instant, awareness washed over her, wiping away her thoughts. Her stranger was here. Halfway across the lobby, she stopped dead in her tracks. Scanning, she found him sitting at a table in the middle of a lounge area. Watching her.

Diego. She said his name in her head. She didn't mean to. It just came to her. Almost as if he had planted it there. Their gazes locked, the connection so intense, she could hardly breathe. His dark eyes seemed to speak to her. Any minute, she expected to hear him. But then he didn't have to speak. Even without words, she knew what he was telling her. He wasn't leaving without her. Logic said she should be scared. Reality said she was more afraid of how wet and wanting he made her. It wasn't normal, this immediate, needy ache he induced. His eyes flared, hot with a sensual appeal, as if he read her thoughts. Head swimming, she wasn't sure if he had touched her mind or not.

He had the ability — of that she was sure. More like her than anyone she had ever met, he had special gifts.

"Marcella, honey, over here."

It was her aunt. Marcella turned towards her voice, waving as she spotted her in a nearby chair. But she couldn't resist one more glance at Diego. Her eyes went towards him, hungry for another fill.

But he was gone.

Disappointment settled into her gut like a heavy load. She shook her head, physically trying to shake her reaction. "This is crazy," she mumbled under her breath as she started walking. He was playing some kind of mind trick on her. He had to be. No one reacted to a stranger the way she was to this man. Perhaps he had a way of shielding himself so she couldn't see the true darkness of his nature.

That had to be it.

She needed to stay away from him.

* * * * *

Marcella followed her aunt into the hotel room. "I'm getting too old for these adventures of yours, dear."

Her aunt sat down on one of the two beds in the room with a heavy sigh. Flowers decorated the covering in bright colors. The room did nothing to calm Marcella's nerves. Even the curtains were a bright orange.

She shut the door and smiled. "Ah, now you and I both know that's not so," Marcella scolded. "You stayed up all night playing dominos with David. He's a bad influence, that man."

She chuckled. "You found me out. I didn't think you knew we were still awake."

Marcella waggled a finger at her. "You know better. I see all and know all."

If only that were true. Sometimes her visions failed her, and often they came after the fact or too late to prevent what was to come. Her true talent was her ability to heal. One she knew came from God—meant to help others. But in the wrong hands, her power could be dangerous. Not everyone was meant to be healed. God had a plan, and she knew when she was to act.

She felt it.

A knock sounded on the door. Marcella found herself taking a few steps backwards to allow entrance. "Who is it?"

A familiar voice. "Me, David."

She opened the door and stood back to let him enter, shutting it again as he passed. "News?"

He leaned against the oak dresser. "Yes, I'm afraid the family's been delayed. It looks like tomorrow morning will be the soonest you can see the child."

Instantly, Marcella thought of Diego. Even if she had planned to meet him—which she hadn't—this would make it impossible.

Aunt Catherine looked worried. "A delay seems strange. You don't think this is some plot to capture Marcella, do you?"

Marcella moved to the bed across from her and sat down. "Don't worry, Aunt. It's not."

Catherine rejected her answer. "It's impossible to be certain." She looked at David. "Please be extra cautious. I have a bad feeling."

"Being nervous is understandable. After all, Marcella lives in danger but I do think things are on the up and up. We did a lot of checking before Marcella agreed to this meeting."

"I had to come." Marcella's heart tightened just thinking about the family. The parents had lost two other children in a car accident a year before. Now they were on the verge of losing another to cancer. They needed their daughter to survive.

"It's dangerous for you to be out like this," Catherine reminded her.

This was not the first time she had had this discussion with her aunt. "I was given a gift meant to be used for good. If I hide my life away I can never give what I am meant to share." She paused. "And I know you agree."

Catherine sighed. "I know." Weariness settled into her features. "And I know you need quiet to meditate," she offered. "I will join David in his room until later tonight."

She reached for the phone. "And I'll order room service so you can eat before you rest."

Nodding, Marcella tried to smile, but her thoughts were heavy with the grief of the parents. She could feel their nearness. It was a comforting feeling she felt often. At times, she even felt they were with her. So far out of reach, but then, so close. And she knew they feared for their daughter. Meditation helped center her powers before a healing session. Under the circumstances, it felt more necessary than usual.

"Thank you," she said in a low voice, trying not to sound distracted. She had to figure what to do about Diego. What if he came for her? Correction, what was she going to do *when* he came for her?

Because he would.

Thirty minutes later, Marcella swallowed the last of a bagel and flipped off the light. She slipped out of her clothes, leaving on her bra and panties. Looking for a gown was too much effort, yet she needed to be comfortable. The curtains were drawn and evening was upon them, making the room dark enough to mimic night. Forcing herself to stretch out on the bed, she tried to blank out her mind. As Diego slipped into her thoughts, she forced him away. One, two, three times…filling her mind with the world of colors she saw as she healed. Over and over, she watched them swim circles in her head…until she sunk into the depth of a deep sleep.

* * * * *

Sitting on his bed, a room service cart in front of him, Diego ate the last bite of his second hamburger. Sometimes, the way he was forced to feed his metabolism was a chore. Reaching for his glass of orange juice, he smiled. Thanks to Holly Heart, the wife of their leader, he would soon give up his dependency on orange juice. The only female who had been enhanced and a brilliant scientist, she had worked in the lab at his side. They were close to perfecting an injection to combat the vitamin C deficiency that haunted the GTECHS. The next step would be figuring out how to use that very same deficiency against the enemy. The men who fought the Arions who had not undergone enhancements needed some sort of way to even the playing field.

He took a sip of his juice. If they could somehow zap the Arions' C levels even further… He shoved the thought aside and set his glass down. First things first. The men who had special powers needed to learn to use them as effectively as the Arions had. Having been on the inside of the Arion operation at one point, Diego knew they had received Alien training. They had also made fast work of recruiting those with special skills such as Marcella's. People who could teach them new things or help them in some way. Either the person joined them or they were disposed of.

The Arions wanted her for two reasons. So the Knights couldn't learn from her, and in hopes she would mate with one of their soldiers. But she was his. Nothing they did could change that. He felt the weight of urgency for so many reasons. To protect Marcella. To help his people.

If only he understood the breeding process more. The Arions didn't either and they went at it like criminals. They simply kidnapped the women they hoped would give them children, holding them in camps awaiting their perfect match.

But right now, Marcella was his concern. The Black Knights hoped Marcella could help them learn to harness the mental capabilities gifted to them. His people needed her.

The Arions wanted her.

She belonged to him.

* * * * *

Marcella.

Her name was like a whisper in her head, barely breaking the depth of her sleep. Yet it was there, sliding into her mind.

Marcella.

Her lids opened instantly. She blinked, eyes slowly adjusting to the darkness, allowing her to focus.

Marcella.

Sitting up, hands beside her, she searched the room. For him. Knowing it was Diego. She found him sitting in the corner chair. Shadows darkened his features, making his eyes impossible to see. But she felt his stare, burning her with its heat. A shudder raced down her spine, but not from fear. It was anticipation.

He pushed to his feet and stepped forward, out of the shadows. Naked and aroused, he was nothing shy of perfection. For some elusive reason, his lack of clothes didn't seem strange. It felt right. With each step he took, her stomach fluttered and her body heated. Almost as if a tiny ball of fire was turning faster and faster.

As he moved to the edge of the bed, pressing his knees into the mattress, she watched with mesmerized appreciation. Both her body and mind seemed to call to him. His presence felt as if it was an answer to her need.

His hand slid to the side of her face, sending a rush of sensation through every nerve ending of her body. "You belong to me." The possessiveness of his words wrapped around her like a warm blanket, offering comfort. His voice, a deep baritone, insinuated into her mind like an added aphrodisiac.

She didn't question the truth of his words. As pure as snow, she knew they were a creation of his very soul. Her hand covered his where it warmed her cheek. The connection she felt to him was beyond this world. Yet she couldn't quite grasp why. "You came."

He was closer now, pulling her into his arms, his body enclosing hers. His hands on her back. Her lips parted in invitation, yearning for the first touch of his mouth. His head lowered his face so near hers, he breathed with her, in and out, as if they were one.

"Please," she whispered, her voice holding a breathless, husky quality. What she was asking for went beyond the kiss she desired. As if there was a void she couldn't fill without him.

His answer was the brush of his lips over hers in a feather-light caress. The touch, though soft, came with an explosive impact. It felt as if her blood had turned to fire, moving through her body and creating a sizzle from the inside out. It spread from head to toe like a blanket of desire.

Unable to wait, she pressed her lips to his, sliding her tongue into his mouth and slowly stroking his. A low growl erupted from his throat as his hand slid to the back of her head, and he kissed her with a hunger born of pure passion. Long, sultry and hot, the kiss pulled her under the spell of the moment, drugging her with its perfection. Her nipples ached for his touch, burning with a bittersweet need.

Side by side now, bodies pressed together, his erection settled between her thighs and teased her with its presence. She wanted him inside her. So much so that a slow burn formed between her legs. Touching and tasting, they molded their bodies together, trying to become one. The same need that drove her seemed to be working its magic on him as well. Her bra was tossed aside, and her nipples pressed into the dark hair of his chest. Wrapping her arms around him, she pressed into him, chest to chest, kissing him, drinking him in.

He was so gentle, yet there was something almost primal in the way he held her. In the passionate way his mouth moved from her lips to her neck and then finally to her breast. His tongue swirled the stiff peak as her hands settled in his hair, a moan slipping from her lips as her lashes fluttered.

Lost. She was so damn lost in the moment. When he nudged her legs apart and slipped between her knees, she felt her heart kick into double time. Her panties were gone and she didn't even remember him taking them off. Maybe she had. Ready to have him inside her, she opened for him, inviting him to slip his cock into hot, wet recesses. The ache she felt for him was almost painful in its brilliance.

But that completion she needed, that she knew he did as well, was yet to come. His mouth settled on her stomach, his hands palming her breasts. Lips, teeth, tongue teased her sensitive skin as his hands slid down her ribs to her hips and around her cheeks.

By the time his mouth covered her clit, she was arching towards him, helping him get to her. For a moment his mouth simply lingered on her sensitive nub, making her moan with the urgency of wanting more. Then with a soft suckle he began to please, tasting her with delicate little strokes of his tongue. One of his fingers slid along her wet folds, adding to the flavor of what he did to her. Provoking an even hotter burn.

Gradually he licked her faster, harder, dipping his tongue into the depths of her core and pushing her further towards the edge of satisfaction. She squirmed beneath him, begging for that ultimate satisfaction. Her fingers dug into the blankets, her head twisted from side to side.

She called out to him. "Please, Diego." She wanted to scream, but in a split second, her voice was gone. A light perspiration formed on her skin as her body screamed for release. As if he knew she could take no more, he suckled her nub as he slid a finger inside her, stroking her inner wall as his mouth did sensual, delicious things.

"Oh," she said. Once, twice. She wasn't sure how many times. Then her body tensed as the very first ripple of orgasm approached, her breath lodging in her throat. Suddenly, she was there, shaking from the intensity of the spasms. From the pleasure that seemed to inch through every nerve ending in her body. And with gentle perfection, he stroked, and kissed, and licked slowing as she did, easing her into relaxation.

And satisfaction.

She let her eyes fall shut, waiting for him to slide up her body, anticipating his hard length sliding inside her slick readiness. A knock sounded on the door. She jumped, a small sound escaping her lips. Rising up on her elbows, she blinked.

Because Diego was gone.

Eyes wide, she searched the room, ignoring the knocking that had started again. Had it been a dream? Her hand slid down her stomach, between her legs, touching the wetness that he had created. The slickness of arousal proved her body's response. But did it prove his presence?

He'd been there. She was sure of it. She pulled the sheet to her shoulders. God, had she dreamed the whole thing? Had she made up something so vivid in her mind that her body had responded?

"You okay in there?" David called through the door.

She cleared her throat. "Yes, fine. Be there in a minute."

"You yelled or something. You sure?"

"Uh…yeah…dream," she responded, her voice hoarse.

Or was it?

Chapter Three

ஐ

At eleven forty-five that night, Marcella tiptoed to the door, trying not to wake her aunt. It had been a tough few hours as she struggled with not only the vividness of her dream but also the reality of the approaching midnight hour. If she didn't go to Diego, she was quite certain he would come to her. A sure disaster. Any number of things could happen if he showed up. David being a major concern. He would confront Diego. Or maybe the opposite. Diego would confront David. Either way it was a no win situation. She had to find Diego before he found her.

As she reached for the door, her aunt's voice stilled her movement. "Marcella, honey, where are you going?"

Inwardly cringing, she turned. "I can't sleep. I'm going to the piano bar downstairs."

Sitting straight up, her aunt shook her head. The light came on. "No. You can't do that. It's not safe." She reached for the phone. "Let me get David to go with you."

"No!" Marcella said, stepping towards her.

"Why?" Catherine asked, confusion in her voice. "That's his job."

"I don't want to wake him. I'm fine. I won't be long." She hoped she sounded convincing.

Apparently not. "That's crazy. You can't go alone." She reached for the phone again.

"Wait!" They stared at each other. In a softer voice, Marcella reached for as close to the truth as possible. She hated lying but she didn't want to cause concern either. "I'm meeting the man from beside the hotel today."

Catherine stilled. After a moment, she sat the receiver down on the base. "Do you know this man?" No accusation in her voice. Only concern.

One of the things Marcella loved about her aunt was her understanding and supportive nature. "I know him," she said, feeling deep in her heart she spoke honestly.

"I wondered when I saw you talking today. I assume you have reasons for leaving David out of this." It wasn't a question.

Marcella smile. "I do."

Catherine's brow's dipped. "I still don't like the idea of you leaving this room unprotected."

"I won't be. He will be waiting on me." And she believed her words.

"I still don't like this." She searched Marcella's face. "I know you though. This is important or you wouldn't be doing it. Who is he to you and why don't I know him?"

Marcella took a deep breath. "I can't explain now. I really have to go, but I promise to tell you everything when I get back."

She hesitated. "How long will you be gone? Decide now because if you are one minute late I am sending David after you."

Marcella smiled. "Thank you, Aunt Catherine. One hour. I will return in one hour."

Seconds passed as if she was contemplating. Then Catherine gave a nod. "One hour."

* * * * *

They'd shared the same dream.

It was a common occurrence once mates had met but not fully joined. Nature wanted them to complete their connection. Even knowing this, the vividness of what they had experienced had astounded him. He could still smell her soft, floral scent. Still taste her on his lips. Just thinking about her made his cock hard. Inwardly, he cursed. His mind needed to be clear to protect her.

Focused on his primal need to take her, he wouldn't be as sharp. In other words, he didn't have time to win her affections. She would want him as he did her. He'd be honest about what their mating meant. He wanted no lies between them. But then he would take her. Make her his. Bury himself deep inside her and tear down the urgency his body and soul created.

Standing in the shadows, he used his keen night vision to take her in with intricate detail. She walked through the hotel doors, hair piled on top of her head, baring the glorious ivory skin of her neck. Eyeing her surroundings, Marcella stopped just beyond the entranceway. Fingers twisting together in front of her, she was clearly nervous. He expected as much under the circumstances. She knew she was hunted.

By him and by others.

Reaching for her with his mind, he sent her a message. *In the trees to your left.*

Her gaze shifted to his location, eyes narrowing. So easily they communicated without words. He'd never experienced such a thing yet he did it with her without thought.

To his surprise, she responded back using her mind. *I'm not going into the woods. I'm going into the lobby. I will wait for you there.* And then she turned and went back into the hotel.

Diego didn't know if he should curse or laugh.

Admittedly, he was from the old Hispanic school of life. His mother was a traditional woman who devoted her life to doing what her husband bid. His father, God rest his soul, had been a brilliant doctor who had worked too much. But his mother never complained. Not once. At least, not in public.

Diego had always dated Hispanic women, mostly because it was what he felt was expected. Now, he was faced with a mate who was not only white but loaded with defiance. A small laugh escaped his lips as he started to walk. Life with his white woman was going to be interesting.

After no more than two steps, he froze. His senses picked up the nearness of at least one Arion. Which meant they knew he was near as well. They could track one another above ground. Only the coverage of underground caverns allowed the Knights to hide from the enemy. And once they had Marcella's presence memorized, they would be able to track her as well. Moving again, this time with urgency, he needed to get to Marcella.

No. It was too late. The Arions were close. He needed to lure them away from her. His presence had been identified. Hers, he was certain, was still doubted or they would have already made a move to take her.

Turning back towards the blackness of the woods, utilizing his exceptional night vision, he sent out a mental call to the enemy. Walking until he was out of sight of the hotel, he stopped, closed his eyes and focused on calling the Arions to him. There was no guarantee they would answer, but his gut said they would.

His hand slid to his waist where he held a gun armed with tranquilizer darts. It was damn hard to kill an Arion with a gun. You had to shoot them in the head just right. But thanks to Holly, they had a new method for battle. Arions who were shot with tranquilizers experienced a temporary loss of powers.

The wind picked up, gushing around him, and he knew the enemy answered his call with a show of their power. Arions, like GTECHS, could travel with the wind. Two Arions appeared, standing side by side. As quickly as it had stirred, the air stilled. Diego took quick stock of the enemy, preparing to battle. Arions loved to fight. It was their first instinct. Kill now. Talk later. And when they came in pairs, they planned for battle.

The bigger of the two had long black hair and a huge scar down his chiseled face. The other, his opposite, sported equally long blond hair. He was short but stout with a rounder face and a red tone to his skin.

The one with black hair spoke. "This isn't Knight territory. Why are you here?"

That he was questioned at all said a lot. They had a purpose they couldn't afford to set aside for battle. And that purpose was finding Marcella.

"I'm here to see family," Diego explained. "I'm alone, not looking for trouble."

The Arion responded fast. "What family?"

"My grandmother."

"You came alone to Mexico to visit your grandmother." It was a flat statement. Disbelief laced his words.

Diego laughed. "I *am* Mexican, in case you didn't notice." His words were meant as a taunt.

Anger flared in the dark ones eyes. "Answer the question."

He needed to get to Marcella. It was all he could think about. "She's ill and I'm a doctor."

The other Arion spoke. "We know who you are. You used to be the Arion doctor."

"Things change," Diego responded.

The short one stepped forward. "You're a damn traitor." His tone held the bite of pent-up violence.

The dark one lifted a staying hand, giving him a sideways glance. "Let it be. We have bigger things to attend." Then he focused on Diego. "Your grandmother is here at this hotel?"

Careful to weave a tale that wouldn't backfire, he thought through his options before answering. "No, but she is meeting me nearby in the morning."

The dark Arion seemed to consider his options. "I'm going to come looking for you tomorrow. You better be gone."

Oh, he would be, and so would Marcella. "Done."

He and the dark Arion locked gazes, a hint of challenge in their exchange. Diego made damn sure his message was clear. He was more than willing to fight. Though he was by nature a healer, he didn't shy away from a battle. He'd long ago learned surviving the Arions meant combat.

The two Arions backed away, the wind kicking dirt into the air at their command.

And then they were gone.

* * * * *

Marcella paced the small, deserted lobby. Okay, so Diego clearly didn't take orders well. Not that she thought he would. She'd reacted out of discomfort. Being outside had felt dangerous. More so than usual. Instinct had kicked in. And it wasn't Diego who had made her feel so concerned. It had been a feeling of darkness.

As if someone or something other than her stranger lurked nearby.

Too much time had passed with no sign of Diego. Maybe he was expecting her to go back outside. She didn't know what to do.

The lone desk clerk, an elderly Hispanic man, eyed her with concern. "Anything you need, señorita?"

"No," Marcella said, forcing a light tone. "Just waiting on a friend."

As if on cue, Diego walked through the door, looking big, bold and far too sexy for Marcella's resistance to hold. She wanted this man like some sort of hunger that demanded to be fed. He stood in the entranceway looking like sin itself, but there was also some sort of Spanish warrior feel about the way he held himself. There was an edge to him. It charged through the air and wrapped around her like some sort of warning.

And then he was walking towards her. With long strides, he closed the distance between them. He moved so fast, she blinked and he was in front of her. He stopped so near she could have leaned forward and touched him.

And she wanted to, but he did it for her. His hand closed around hers, warm and secure.

She looked up at him, feeling the impact in her stomach. A flutter of awareness. A flash of the moments in her dream, naked, bodies pressed together. His eyes heated in return, and she felt the fire of the shared experience as if it was happening again. He had the same memory. There was no time to anticipate her response. She leaned into him, feeling an uncontrollable urge to be close to him. She replayed his words from her dream.

You belong to me.

At that moment, she thought it just might be true. She of all people knew there were things in life that couldn't be explained. Things that simply were. There were also things created by greater powers. And though those things frightened most, they simply were reality to her.

Whatever was happening between her and this man was a part of a higher power.

"Marcella." His voice was low. Sensual. Even urgent.

"Yes?" she asked, her eyes probing his features. He was wound tight. Ready for…battle perhaps?

He opened his mouth to speak and then shut it again. "Come with me." Already on the go, he pulled her with him.

Having no option but to follow, his hand still firmly holding hers, she scrambled to keep up without running. "Where are we going?"

He didn't answer until they stopped at the elevators. "My room."

She swallowed. "That's not a good idea." They both knew what would happen if they were alone.

The doors opened. "Neither is standing here in the open." Not waiting for a reply, he led her inside the car and punched the button for his floor.

The doors closed leaving them alone and silent. She quivered with the richness of her feelings. For him. This stranger. It was best to talk to him now, before she went into his room. She turned to face him. Dark eyes met hers, possessive and hungry. Her words disappeared.

He leaned against the wall and pulled her close. As if he was protecting her. It was the oddest thing for a stranger to do. Yet...it felt right. Safe. Perfect. Her hand rested on his chest, her body close to his, heat radiating through his clothes. Burning her with a promise for more.

Silence. The ding of floors as they passed. The "what ifs" lacing the air.

When the doors opened, he gently urged her to exit, taking her hand as if he couldn't risk losing her. She didn't want to leave. Maybe it was in another lifetime or another realm, but she knew this man in a soul-deep way. She belonged here with him. Logical it wasn't. Reality it was.

* * * * *

Diego pushed open the hotel door, eager to get Marcella out of the public eye for more reasons than one. She entered the room without hesitation. Following, he let the door shut behind him. He didn't bother with the light. The curtains were open, and the moon full. The room glowed with its brilliance, perfect in its seductive play of shadows.

His body yearned for what only Marcella could give him, and he saw no reason to deny what was inevitable. They were meant to be together, bound by body and soul.

She knew it as well as he did. He felt her response. Felt her acceptance. The door shut behind her. He allowed her to walk past him, his nostrils flaring with the soft scent she wore. Jasmine.

He flipped the locks but didn't follow her. He simply watched. Turning to face him, she met his gaze, saying nothing. Her eyes, and perhaps her mind, reached for answers he wanted to give. But their time was limited. The Arions were near, and he needed her. His mind and soul reached for her. His body demanded he take her.

He leaned against the door, butt against the hard surface, feet slightly spread. Willing himself to keep his hands off her until they talked. "You're not afraid of me." It wasn't a question. He felt it.

"Should I be?" she asked, one brow lifting in challenge.

"You know the answer," he countered, a slight twitch to his lips.

She seemed to consider his words. He felt the brush of her mind in his own. Even welcomed it. And then felt the emptiness of her pulling back before she agreed. "I'm not afraid of you."

"There are things you need to know," he said, "and quickly. We cannot stay here much longer."

"I can't leave yet," she said, firmness to her voice. "The little girl won't arrive until tomorrow. I can't leave her."

She wasn't refusing to go with him. Her subconscious mind was leaving an opening. She wanted to be with him. He saw that as a positive. With their connection came a sense of belonging. He expected her to resist, but in the end she would come with him. She had to. And deep in his heart he wished he had the time to win her in the right way. As a human woman, she needed time. Something he didn't have to offer.

"When tomorrow?" he asked.

She sat down on the bed, making his view of her expressions impossible. "Early morning."

He pushed off the door, wanting to see her face as they talked. Stopping in front of her, he leaned on the dresser. "This is important to you."

Her fingers dug into the floral bedspread as she nodded. Their eyes met. "Yes. Of course. It's a little girl."

His tone was soft, but his words dictated. He understood her concern, but he also had to think about the future of humanity. "We can't stay longer than early morning. If she isn't here, we must leave."

Defiance laced her response. "I'm not leaving without helping her."

"You are in grave danger."

She laughed without humor. "That isn't anything new."

"You have never faced an enemy like this one. Nothing you have ever been up against has prepared you for what lies before us now."

She wet her lips, drawing his eyes to her sensual mouth and making his cock harden. Damn, this was difficult. He wanted to fuck her. To possess her. Then later, he would make slow love to her. There was no way to stop the wildness of his raging body. The urgent need to claim his mate was like boiling liquid in his veins.

"Explain," she said, her voice a bit breathless as if she felt the calling of her body too.

He walked to the window, staring out into the darkness, his back to her. A minute to cage the roar of desire was necessary. When he felt he was a bit more in control, he spoke. But he didn't turn to face her. He couldn't. Not and be certain of his restraint. "The government conducted a scientific experiment. They used findings from Area 51 to enhance the abilities of an elite group of soldiers. They injected the men with a serum and told them it was vaccinations."

"But it wasn't," she said softly.

He forced himself to turn and face her, knowing she needed to see the truth in his eyes. "No, it wasn't." He paused, giving her a minute to search his expression. "It was a genetics experiment. Alien DNA mixed with human DNA."

Her eyes widened, and he watched her delicate white throat bob. "Alien DNA." It wasn't a question. It was more a statement of shock.

"The results were as expected. Super Soldiers were exactly what they created. The men involved became stronger, more powerful."

"Are you one of those Super Soldiers?"

"Yes, but we are now divided in two groups which come down to the basics of life, good and evil. The Black Knights, the good, and the Arions, the evil."

"Which are you?" she challenged.

Something primitive flared. His woman should not challenge him. "You know the answer to that."

Her brow inched upward. "Do I?"

Closing the distance between them, he took several long strides and dropped to his knees in front of her. His hands rested on the tops of her thighs, her thin skirt the only barrier between his hand and her skin. The touch was like an explosion of heat. Her scent wafted him with its soft, sensual aroma. Calling to him deep in his soul like a commanding roar.

"You know I'm not evil," he told her. "You know me."

Her hands went to his wrists, but she didn't push him away. "How can I possibly know you?"

Her words showed resistance but contradicted her actions. Her upper body swayed towards him, her lips parted, her eyes darkening. His hands slid down her calves and then back up her legs, beneath her skirt. She sucked in a breath.

"Diego." She said his name as if it was a question.

He answered by gently easing her knees apart, fitting himself in the V of her legs. Her hands slid to her sides, fingers digging into the blanket as if she fought the urge to touch him. She sucked in a breath as he pressed his body against hers. "You belong to me." One of his hands slipped from beneath her skirt, sliding up her side, following the curve of her sultry form to her back. Pressing her closer to him, easing her full breasts into his chest. He felt her shiver. "I know you feel our connection."

Her hands went to his shoulders "Yes," she whispered, "but why? I don't know why."

Lips lingering just above hers, he could almost taste her without touch. "One mate for life," he explained, feeling the possessiveness of knowing she was that to him. "You are that person for me. I cannot live without you."

"This is crazy," she whispered, her voice holding a breathless quality. "I shouldn't be here. How can I respond to a stranger like this? So…"

"Potent," he said, but it wasn't a question. It was merely giving voice to what he felt. His mouth closed down on hers, needing what only she could give. The first touch of her soft lips melted him inside out. He was on fire yet he felt relief, as if a flame had been sprayed with water and ignited at the same time.

His tongue slid past her teeth, soaking in her flavor with one deep stroke and then another. How he managed to be gentle he wasn't sure. The last thing he wanted was to scare her. The beast inside begged to be unleashed yet somewhere, somehow, he found the will to contain it. For her.

But the beast would only wait so long.

Chapter Four

ഇ

Never, ever had she felt so consumed. So possessed. So ready to give herself. Desperate to get a grip on what was happening, she reached deep and pressed her palms against Diego's chest. Their lips parted. It was what she wanted, yet it wasn't. She had to fight the urge to pull his mouth back to hers. Reaching for restraint, she reminded herself how much she needed answers. She had to have answers.

"Talk to me," she said breathlessly. "What is happening to me?" She paused. "To us?"

His forehead found hers, his breathing heavy like hers. "You are my mate. The only woman I can ever desire." He paused. "I need you."

The intense emotion in his voice made her pull back to look at him. The dark depths of his eyes, the heat, the fire, the need, made her suck in a breath. The crazy part was she wanted him to touch, taste and…take her. No, not wanted. Needed. She needed him.

Her voice was a whisper as she struggled to find words. "How…how can this be happening?"

His hand slid to the side of her face, gently cupping it. "I want to give you time to think about all of this," he paused, seeming to hesitate. "Please believe me when I say this. Yet…the truth is," another pause, "I can't."

She leaned back a bit. The word "can't" didn't seem like one he would use. "Why?"

"Once a male of my kind finds his mate, the need to become one with that person consumes. It is like a fire that burns hotter with each passing moment. For the male it can be almost crippling."

Swallowing, she tried to digest his words. The implications were so extreme they were hard to comprehend let alone reconcile in her mind. Refusing to panic over what could be a misunderstanding, she decided she needed more clarification. Was he referencing the DNA changes made to him and others? He spoke as if he was of another race. "Your kind? What exactly does that mean?"

Ignoring her direct question, he continued explaining his physical needs. "I need to be bound to you to be at my best," he said. "Our enemy is near, and it is you they seek." His eyes darkened, and then he added, "To fight at my full ability, I need you."

Fear sent a shiver down her spine. But she wasn't afraid of Diego. It was this unknown enemy. As crazy as it all sounded, she knew he spoke the truth. Someone was after her. And he was here to protect her.

His hand slid to her face so that he cradled it in his palms, and he responded to her silent worries. "I will never let anything happen to you."

"Why me?" she whispered, mind racing with turbulent thoughts. "Why do they want me?"

"You know the answer," he said in a gentle voice. "Your gifts have always made you a target. It's simply a new enemy."

She closed her eyes, fighting a multitude of emotions. She wanted Diego, and in the same moment she feared for her safety. After several deep breaths she looked at him again. "You said you must be bound to me to be at your best. Explain."

His hands slid to her neck and then shoulders. He leaned towards her, his lips brushing her temple. She felt the soft touch from head to toe, a rush of pure sensation. Need. Yearning…to touch him. She had to. Her hands went to his chest. How she had kept from touching him until this moment she hadn't a clue.

Her palms found his chest, fingers spreading wide as she tried to absorb him. His dark eyes, black as night, met hers, seeming to pull her closer to him even though he didn't move. Her skin pebbled with goose bumps as if he had touched her with his look.

His muscles flexed beneath her palm and a small sound escaped her lips. Where it came from she didn't know. Everything was happening as if a larger-than-life force controlled her. One that made her feel beyond the moment. Beyond time.

"Tell me," she whispered, not saying more. Knowing it wasn't necessary. He knew what she meant. Her gaze dropped to his mouth. Full, sensual lips parted as if in invitation. She forced her eyes back to his, her tongue absently stroking her bottom lip. "I need to know." The words came out like a choked plea. One she felt with desperation. Whatever this thing was between them, she wanted to understand it. Maybe then she could get a grip on herself. Yes. She needed to understand.

Diego's knuckles caressed her cheek. "I can never love another." Sincerity laced his voice. "Only you. To be this near you and not claim you as my own will weaken my powers. Under other circumstances, I would expect to let you get used to this idea." He paused. "But there simply is no time. We must act."

As if this stranger could really love her, a woman he had only just met. "Claim me as your own?" She laughed, though it was without humor. He'd meant his words. Truth always echoed in her mind, as did lies. It was one of her talents. One that often came with pain. Sometimes one didn't want to know when someone was feigning niceties.

She squeezed her eyes shut again, trying to block out what must be a dream. "This can't be real." Desire took hold, hot, like fire in her veins, barely contained. It was with an iron will she fought the need to press her body against his. She could feel her nipples, hard and achy against her bra, begging for his hands...his mouth.

Diego's hand settled at her waist. "Look at me, Marcella."

She took a deep breath and did as he requested. No, demanded. He seemed to claim power over her. Their eye contact made her stomach flutter. Her fingers clenched his shirt. "I belong to no one."

The warmth of his hands moved from her wrists to her upper arms. It took her off guard, and she found herself unable to respond. And then his lips, those sexy, perfect lips, brushed hers.

His mouth lingered a breath away, just out of reach. "We belong to each other," he whispered. "I know you can feel it."

His mouth caressed hers again, and this time she couldn't fight the urgency of her own need. Her fingers slid into his hair as she pressed her lips to his. Not willing to accept brief contact. Their mouths seemed to melt into one another, absorbing. For long seconds they stayed that way, bodies somehow pressing closer, arms wrapping each other's bodies.

His forehead met hers again, a gesture seeming more intimate each time he did it. "Tell me you feel it."

Her palm went to his cheek. "You already know I do."

One second…two. Suddenly, his mouth slanted over hers, his tongue sliding against hers in a hot, demanding possession. Responding was as instant as her next breath. She tasted him like sweet nectar, drinking greedily of his unique flavor. Everything she knew as her world slipped into the darkness of her passion.

It didn't matter that her blouse and bra were somehow on the floor. What mattered was his hand, now on her breast. His fingers tweaked her nipple, answering her body's cry for his touch. His mouth trailed her neck, her chin, and then found her lips again.

Impatient, she kissed him while tugging at his shirt, wanting to feel his skin. No. It was a need. She needed to be pressed against him, to be as close as possible. He leaned back and pulled the shirt over his head. Dark hair sprinkled his chest, his warm brown skin like an aphrodisiac.

She reached for him, wanting to kiss him again. His hands went to her arms, his breath heavy enough to be heard. As if he was straining to contain his desire. "I am near a point of no return, Marcella. Once we do this, we are bound for life. I need to know you want what I am offering you. My protection. My love. And," he said in a deeper voice, "my life."

Deep somewhere inside she knew this was all crazy. It didn't seem real. It was a dream. And she wanted what he offered. Maybe it was nothing more than the heat of the moment, but that second, she would not have denied him anything.

"I want this," she whispered, feeling a comfort in the words that went beyond saying them. "Make love to me." Their eyes locked, and she saw his pupils grow, taking up almost all of the white in his eyes. Inside her mind, and perhaps her very soul, she felt a different side of him surface. More...animalistic. More primal. Yet she wasn't afraid.

Calling him to her was like a cry from her innermost self. "Now, Diego," she said. "Take me now."

* * * * *

Desire. Raw, red-hot, burning desire. It stroked his cock without even a touch. Her silky quality of her words and the anticipation they evoked made him harder than he'd ever been in his life.

"Be certain," he whispered in a hoarse voice. "There is no turning back." Everything inside him raged with the need to take her. Waiting for her answer felt like years as she reached deep for restraint. Though he didn't have time for her to understand fully what was happening, he most definitely wanted her to make the choice...to trust him. To give herself to her mate.

Her delicate little hands slid under his arms and up his back, her nipples pressing into his chest in an unspoken invitation reinforced by her words. Chin tilted upward, lips parted, she gave him a sultry look. "Make love to me, Diego."

No hesitation, his mouth captured hers in a passionate kiss. It was as if the beast inside had been waiting, ready to claim its feast. Never before in his life had he needed like he needed in that moment. Suddenly, they were clinging to one another, hands exploring, tongues tangling, bodies pressed close. But he wanted more. Hands beneath the round perfection of her ass, he moved her so that she was flat in the center of the mattress.

Urgency drove his hands as he shoved her skirt up and pushed her knees apart. He settled his groin into the center of her body's V, still kissing her, his tongue lapping at hers as if he was drinking her very life. Instead, he was finding his own.

Her body arched into his, driving him wild as she squirmed beneath him, hands traveling his body with tantalizing caresses. He moaned, the scrape of her nails down his flesh drawing not a sound of pain but a sound of pleasure. The roar of his darker side wanted to be fed, and Marcella's wild abandonment only made him thirst for more.

He palmed her breast, kneading it, squeezing, pinching the nipple. She made a soft purr. Her breathing was heavy, her chest rising and falling. His lips traveled to her neck, teeth scraping the sensitive skin even as his other hand fingered and pinched a pink, perfect nipple.

"Oh God, Diego. What are you doing to me?" She gasped the words, her hands on his head, her nipple erect under the sweet play of his touch. His mouth found the red bud and suckled. Her hips arched into his, and he pressed into her in response, a sudden urgency to be inside her claiming him. But not like this. Not with their clothes on.

While he still had the will, he pulled himself off her, standing at the end of the bed and reaching for the button of his jeans. She leaned up, weight on her elbows, breasts full with arousal as she displayed them for his viewing.

"What are you doing?" she asked, her voice heavy with passion.

"Get undressed," he said. "I want to see and feel all of you. Every inch." He bent down and started untying his shoes. She reached for one shoe and tossed it to the floor with a loud thud. He had managed to get rid of one of his by the time she tossed the other. And then she was there, standing above him, skirt falling to the floor, a pool of material at her feet. She stepped out of the garment and kicked it aside. In a slow perusal, his eyes traveled from her perfectly painted pink toenails up the creamy white perfection of her calves, to the thighs he so wanted wrapped around his body. And then her panties fell to the floor.

His eyes followed the small piece of emerald silk, dark green, like the color of her eyes, fell to her feet. But his gaze lingered only a brief instant. Hungrily he focused on the triangle of red curls between her legs. He moved forward, hands sliding up the back of her thighs, cupping her cheeks as his mouth found her mound. She cried out, her hands lacing into his hair. He suckled her bud and then licked and tasted, loving the intimacy of knowing her...his woman.

His fingers slid along the slick folds of her body, caressing, exploring and then slipping inside her. He stroked her inner wall, moving his fingers in simulated sex, making her hips arch, pressing her bud into his mouth. She made a soft sound of pleasure and it drove him crazy, making him lap at her with more hunger.

"Diego," she cried out, "I can't...stand. I—"

He felt her tremble an instant before her knees buckled. Moving both hands around her ass, he firmed his grip, holding her up so she wouldn't fall. All the while his tongue swirled and licked her into satisfied bliss, slowing as she slowed.

The instant she calmed, he urged her onto the bed, but he didn't kiss her as he yearned to do. First things first. He needed to get rid of the remainder of his clothes. Because it was way past time he was inside her.

* * * * *

Marcella had never given sex much thought. Until now. She was shaking. Literally trembling. She could feel her bottom lip quiver. Not from fear from pleasure. From a shared intimacy with a stranger so intense it seemed to turn her insides out. There were things in life that called to her beyond the physical. To feel what she felt now, she knew they existed beyond this experience.

And though her need for Diego had manifested in the form of desire, he too was linked to her beyond this moment. Beyond touch.

He stood at the end of the bed, his cock long and hard, and his eyes wild with a raging inferno. For her. Marcella's eyes lingered on the proof of his arousal. Had he been closer she would have touched him. Wrapped her hand around the width and felt him pulse in her hand.

For now, she settled for looking. And what a sight he was. Tall, broad and packed with lean, sexy muscles in all the right places. He had pecs that begged to be touched and abs that demanded her lips. She'd just had an amazing orgasm and she was all hot and wanting all over again. She wanted him inside her. It pulled at her like a living, growing expectancy.

As if answering her call, he was there, on top of her. His hands pressed her legs apart, fingers sliding into her wetness, preparing her. Then his mouth was there, on hers, tongue probing. He guided his cock to her body, moving it along her aroused core and moaning into her mouth.

And then he sunk deep.

She cried out. He cried out. Together they felt the impact of their joining. His face was buried in her neck, and she felt him shudder though he didn't move. What she experienced in that moment she didn't understand. It was like a shiver rushed through her body. And then she shuddered as he had, ripples of pleasure dancing along her nerve endings with all-consuming pleasure.

He raised his head, one hand sliding into her hair, and looked into her eyes. His mouth lingering so close she could almost taste him. And then as if an animal was unleashed, he was kissing her. Crazy, hot, kissing her and she couldn't get enough. They pressed into each other, moving together, raw with an urgency to get closer.

He rose up on his hands, an amazing, powerful sight, thrusting into her. She wanted to watch him, to take in the sheer force of his beauty. But each stroke, each thrust, hit her with a rush of pleasure. The intensity forced her eyes shut.

Arching upward, she met him with a push. "More," she said or maybe she just thought it. She didn't know. She just wanted. "More. Harder."

A low growl escaped his throat, and he flattened his hard body against her softer one, kissing her even as he pushed deeper. She wrapped her legs around his, pulling her hips into his, kissing him in between moans, touching his face, his back, his shoulders.

And with perfect timing, like an answer to a burning question, he squeezed her breast and pinched her nipple. She arched into him. His hands moved down her sides, around her ass, pulling her tighter against his body. The angle allowed her to take more of him.

"Yes," she moaned breathlessly and tried to press her chest tighter against his. They were so close, bodies touching everywhere, yet it wasn't enough. If she could have crawled under his skin at that moment, she would have. There was desperation to her movements and to his as they twisted and turned together.

In. Out. Sideways. Oh so marvelously, but never, ever, enough. She could never get enough.

He whispered something in Spanish, but she couldn't make out his words. She was too…there. Too on the edge. No. Over the edge. She felt the first spasm of orgasm like she was shattering. Shocked when she lingered on the tip of fulfillment.

Diego called her name, thrusting with fierceness, once again raised up on his hands. But her legs still clung to his, holding him firmly, not letting him escape. She was so damn close to the ultimate pleasure. To the moment. Diego moaned, arching his back and thrusting hard, deep, harder.

And the moment of no return had come. Her hands clenched the sheets, her face moving from side to side. "Oh God," she moaned, feeling like she was about to explode.

An animal-like groan escaped Diego's lips, and he buried himself inside her with completeness like no other stroke. He shuddered as she shattered, her body shaking with the impact. The pleasure so abrupt and bold, she could hardly breathe.

When finally they both stilled, Diego slowly lowered himself, rolling to his side and taking her with him. Holding her, hand stroking her hair with gentleness so unlike the wildness in his lovemaking.

She loved how he felt. How being in his arms made her all warm inside. But even as she lavished in the moment, her head began to spin. A wave of sickness rolled through her body. "Oh. I…" She swallowed, squeezing her eyes shut. "I'm dizzy."

His palm went to her cheek. "Look at me, my love, *mi vida.*"

His voice reached inside her and seemed to calm. She forced her eyes open. "I don't know what's wrong with me."

"It will pass in a few minutes. I promise."

"How do you know?" she whispered, the room spinning.

He kissed her forehead. "It is part of your body binding to mine. It is quite normal."

Inhaling, Marcella willed herself to calm. "What have you done to me?"

* * * * *

He knew this moment would come. But he also knew she would always have a choice. Never would he take that from her. Running his hand down her hair, he tried to comfort. With a slight shift he rolled around to face her.

"I will never want another woman. We are bound body and soul. You, on the other hand, are still human. That hasn't been taken from you. Though you will want me, even need me, you still have the ability to live on without me."

Her eyes were wide now, no longer looking so dazed. "But you can't live without me?"

"I can, yes, but I will never want another." He paused. "And I will forever need you. If you are by my side, I will be stronger in all ways possible."

She blinked several times. "And if I'm not?"

He ignored her question, not wanting to contemplate a separation. And with effort, he made himself ask rather than tell what came next. "My people need me as does the good of humanity so I must return to our base. I hope you will go with me." He paused. "For me. For the better of our planet. We need your help." He ran his finger over her lip. "I need you."

"You didn't answer my question. What happens if I'm not with you?"

It would destroy him, but he wasn't about to admit such a thing. She needed to make this decision herself. To be with him of her own free will. When he didn't respond immediately, she sat up, the sheet falling to her waist, giving him a tantalizing view of her ivory-skinned torso. Pulling her legs to her chest, she pressed her chin to her knees, hair falling forward like a veil of silk.

He was still trying to decide how to answer when his eyes caught and held on the vision on the back of Marcella's neck. His mark. The Arion star. It denoted the mate of an Arion male. His breath caught in his throat. Knowing she was fully his was like a rush. His mark was now a part of her existence from here on out. Love, lust and an array of feelings he couldn't quite decipher swirled inside. And possessiveness. She was his.

She cut him a sideways look. "Well?"

He sat up, wrapping his arms around her waist and pressing his lips to the star. She sucked in a breath, and he knew she felt his emotion. It was potent inside him, reaching for her as a new day did the sun. Because he was a new man because of her.

"What are you doing to me?" she whispered.

"It's already done." He kissed her neck again. "You wear my mark."

She twisted around to see him, grabbing for the sheet and pulling it over her chest. "What?" Then her eyes darted beyond him. "Oh no. Damn it." She crawled over him, reaching for the phone.

Perched half on top of him, her breasts were pressed against his chest. His hand found her hip and his cock stirred. "What are you doing?"

"My aunt is going to be worried sick. I told her I would be back in an hour. It's been two."

His hand slid up to her breast and he fingered her nipple. "Tell her you won't be back tonight."

She moaned at the play of his fingers. "Stop." Receiver in her hand, Marcella looked at him. His brow quirked. He didn't like his woman telling him not to touch her. As if she read his mind, which she well might have, she answered, "I can't concentrate when you touch me like that." A two-second pause. "And I can't tell her that. She'll freak."

She belonged with him. Period. The end. He'd be damned if he was letting her out of his sight. Danger was too close. His hands slid around her waist, his jaw tight with the sudden tension lacing his body. "You're in danger. You stay with me."

Her eyes locked with his, and then to his surprise, she set the receiver down, leaning over him and pressing her lips to his. Then, her eyes full of affection, she trailed her fingers down his cheek. "I feel your concern. I'll be fine. Stop worrying."

His fingers laced into her hair. "You're right. You will be. Because you're staying here with me."

"Diego—" He reached for the phone, shuffling her off to his side. "What are you doing?"

He glanced at her. "I'm calling your aunt."

"What?" she gasped. "No! Give me the phone." But it was too late. Marcella could hear her aunt's voice. "Hello," she said in a worried voice. "Hello. Marcella?"

Diego looked at Marcella, handed her the phone and then spoke to her through their mental connection. *You tell her or I will.*

* * * * *

Marcella's eyes narrowed on Diego, hot with temper. She wanted him to see and feel the anger he'd inspired. With gritted teeth she grabbed the phone from him. "Yes, Aunt, it's Marcella."

"Oh thank God. I've been worried sick. David is searching the hotel. Where are you?"

"I'm safe," Marcella assured her, eyeing Diego. A hint of a satisfied smile played on his too sexy lips. She gave him a warning look but spoke to her aunt. "I'll explain later. Well, tomorrow. Not tonight. Aunt, I'm not coming back to the room tonight."

Silence. She could almost visualize her aunt's jaw hanging open. "David won't like this. He'll demand you return."

Marcella felt the rise of Diego's irritation without him so much as blinking. He had a cool exterior, but it hid nothing from her. The realization came with surprise. She had never felt another's emotion with such ease.

Suddenly, Marcella was both afraid for David and surprisingly warmed by Diego's possessiveness. Delicately, she cleared her throat, feeling a bit overwhelmed with emotion. Something about Diego felt like home. It frightened her how much she wanted to be with a complete stranger.

"Tell David I'll be fine," she said, and in a softer voice, "I will be. I promise. I'm safe." And she knew she was. Diego would protect her. "I'll call in the morning."

A promise wasn't enough. Very worried, her aunt continued to press, desperation slipping into her voice as she pleaded for Marcella's return. Giving her Diego's room number was the final outcome of the conversation.

With a heavy sigh, Marcella hung up the phone. Diego lay on his back, hands behind his head. Oblivious to her nakedness, she crawled over him, straddling his hips and flattening her palms on his chest, fingers nestled in the dark hair. "David's harmless. He's just doing his job."

Diego's eyes lingered on her breast, his hands settling on her hips. "I don't like him or his intentions. The man wants you, Marcella."

She didn't like when he said things like that. Her hands covered his. "Must you be so blunt?"

"If putting the cold hard facts bluntly is what it takes to get your attention, then yes. David's desire for you is blatant yet you choose to ignore it." He slid his hands up her back, pulling her towards him. His fingers slid behind her neck, pulling her lips towards his, their breath mingling. In a softer voice he said, "I protect what is mine."

She tightened her lips, fighting the urge to press her mouth to his, trying to ignore the play of his chest hair on her nipples. "Yes, let's talk about this 'mine' thing you keep saying. I belong to me. If I choose to be with you it's because I *choose* to be with you."

His eyes narrowed. "And do you choose to be with me, Marcella?"

Chapter Five

🔊

The way he said her name, with a sexy little Spanish accent lifting the last vowel, made her stomach flip-flop. His dark eyes locked with hers and held. After several spellbound seconds she looked away. "This is crazy. We're strangers."

He moved then, and she found her back on the mattress, his hard body on top of hers, his legs pinning hers as if he was afraid she might escape. "I know you need time to accept who and what I am to you. As much as I want to demand you accept me, I know I cannot." He brushed his lips across hers in a gentle caress.

She wasn't quite sure what to say. "This is very confusing."

"I must return home with you by my side."

Her eyes went wide. "What? When?" Her mind raced. "Where?"

"Nevada." No hesitation. "As soon as you heal the girl."

"Nevada?" she half gasped. Had she not been trapped under his big body she would already be standing. "I can't just leave. No." She shook her head, feeling a tiny bit of panic.

"You have to, Marcella."

"No, I don't. I don't *have* to do anything."

His eyes flashed with something dark. "Your life and that of many others could depend on you. We feel you can help us in ways no other can."

"How can *I* help? My healing abilities? I won't heal as a part of war. You've picked the wrong woman."

"You are the right woman for many reasons. One of which is our leader's wife. She is with child. It will be the first time a converted human gives birth. She must live. She is the light that keeps our leader focused."

"Are there complications?"

"Not yet, but I'm not prepared to enter the unknown unprepared. Too much is on the line. I need someone by my side. I need you to be that someone." His voice was possessive. Low. They stared at one another a long moment before he added, "This is not about war. It's about peace. Good versus evil. Myself and the men like me, we have abilities we don't know how to fully utilize. The enemy does. It's rumored they actually had an alien race training them. It is quite possible the originator of the DNA used for our enhancement is joining in their battle."

"Why?" she asked, fearing she knew the answer. "Do you know the Arion's motivation?"

"The Arion leader wishes to rule the world. Perhaps he aspires to rule the universe."

She blinked. It was hard enough to think with Diego both naked and on top of her. Add to it a story too wild to conceive, and her head felt clouded. "This is crazy. I feel like I'm in the twilight zone."

"You of all people should understand the realm of possibilities. You have powers others don't. Some believe you're evil. Others say you're simply make-believe. My point being, you are very real and very gifted. What I'm telling you may be hard to comprehend but it is nevertheless quite real."

He was speaking the truth. She could do things normal humans could not. If she possessed such unique skills, how could she reject what she couldn't conceive? Marcella believed Diego. In her heart and soul she trusted him as well. She reached up, her finger tracing his bottom lip. "Tell me more," she whispered.

He smiled, his eyes saying he knew he'd received her acceptance. "We need your help."

"Then I'm right," Marcella said. "It's my healing power you desire?"

"Ah, my sweet," he said, desire suddenly alive in his words, lips brushing her cheek, her jaw, her lips. "It's your body and soul I desire...and your heart."

Her eyes felt heavy, her body warm. His cock was hard, pressing between her thighs. Her body responded, dampness gathering from the need to feel him inside her.

"Diego," she whispered. "Please. I need to understand." His lips brushed hers, his tongue sliding past her teeth and stroking, sucking her into a whirlwind of passion. Marcella forgot for a moment what she was going to say. A pause. Another kiss. She tried to focus, needing answers. "I can't think like this."

His hips moved, sliding his length along her mound, following the trail of wetness. A moan escaped her lips. "Diego."

"I need you, Marcella."

She felt his hands travel her body. No, his mouth. Both. He touched, kissed, nipped. All with sweet, passionate love. It was like nothing she'd ever experienced. Where he had pinched her nipple before, he stroked it with his warm tongue, making her arch her back. Her hands went to his amazing hair. She loved how it felt. How he felt.

The burn where he wasn't, but should be, made her squirm. "I want you inside me."

His head lifted from the nipple he suckled, his eyes dark. Mesmerizing. She stared into them and lost her breath. It was as if he had crawled inside her and wrapped himself around her very soul. She felt an inner touch. An invisible connection. A pleasure of a new kind heated her inside, potent with the impact. His eyelids were heavy and she knew he felt it as well. The words he spoke not long before came to her, "your body is binding to mine".

It was as he said.

They were as one.

His mouth closed down on hers, hungry with its demands, and she moaned against his lips. And then gasped as his cock slid into her body. "Marcella," he whispered.

She felt her name like a caress.

Her body arched, her butt lifting as she pressed her hips against his. All she could think was *closer*. Harder. More. He moved in slow, sensual strokes, in and out of her body. One of his hands playing with her nipple, palming her breast. And then a hard thrust injected her with a rush of pleasure.

"Diego," she rasped.

He held himself above her, palms pressed into the mattress, and slowly, inch by inch, slid backwards, his cock positioned with only the tip inside her. His eyes met hers. For long moments they stared at one another, her breath caught in her throat. Her heart pounding at double time. The room faded away with the force of their joining.

And then, in a slow, sexy progression, he slid back inside her, giving her not just his body but also something beyond. Still holding her stare, she felt his mind open to hers. He buried himself to the hilt and then his face went to her neck. Images rushed through her brain. Flashes of events. Battles. Diego doing surgery. Monsters battling men Diego called friends. A human woman bonding with a man she knew to be the Black Knight's Leader. And then her...naked in Diego's arms as she was now.

Where she belonged.

Suddenly his mouth was on hers, the images replaced by red-hot desire. His hips beginning to move. His long, hard cock stroking her inner walls with back and forth motions. Lost in everything he was, her body reached for his. Her hips lifted from the bed, driven by an absolute need to feel complete. And he was her only hope of making it so.

Diego's lips were like a silky caress, touching her with sensual tenderness, tasting lips, her neck and her shoulder. And then his teeth scraped her shoulder. Sharp but erotic. The pinch of pain she felt somehow only made the next thrust of his cock more amazing. She called out his name, her neck tilting backwards. Her fingers sunk into his back as the pleasure burst and then splintered like a million pieces of bliss shattering through her body.

She shook with the potency of her release, feeling Diego's teeth on her nipples and then his tongue. The touch of his mouth seemed to make another ripple. And another. Until slowly...she stilled. Diego brushed hair out of her face, leaning on his elbow and staring at her with dark, passion filled eyes. "You are so damn beautiful," he murmured.

Her hand went to his fingers, bringing them to her lips and kissing them. "You didn't come," she whispered. "It's your turn."

"I wanted to watch your pleasure," he replied, his voice heavy with passion.

Her body was still squeezing and stroking him, the aftershock of her orgasm intense. "I want to watch you." She suckled his finger into her mouth, her eyes locked with his, begging him to take. Mimicking him, her teeth scraped his finger and then his wrist, hands gliding up his arms.

A low moan escaped his throat just before his mouth claimed hers, and he thrust with power. *Yes*, she whispered to him in her mind. *More.*

She felt the animal in him roar, and she seized the beauty of awakening it. In her heart she saw the wilder part of him, and thrilled at his more animalistic urges. For some reason it made her hot. Burning beyond belief. The more he gave her, thrust after thrust, the more she wanted. Something about this man and all he was charged her with a sexual high she'd never known.

His head lifted, dark hair falling forward, eyes wide. She stared at him, her gaze feasting on the magnificent male perfection that was him. Her man. Her soul mate. She knew it to be so. Wanted it. Accepted. Even burned to feel all it could be. The low groans he made as he thrust echoed in her head and made her press her hips into him, now taking and giving.

But her eyes stayed on his face. She was watching the moment he exploded. The moment the wild roar of complete pleasure ripped from his lungs. "Oh God," she whispered, so completely shaken by what her body, both inside and out, felt. A flutter in her stomach, and then to her utter shock, her body rippled with yet another release. "Diego, I..." Words were lost to pleasure.

They shuddered and shook. When finally they stilled, they lay intimately wrapped together, naked, body and soul as one. And they slept.

* * * * *

A loud pounding on the door made Marcella jump.

Diego raised his head, his body tensing. She could feel the readiness ooze from him. "Marcella, are you in there?"

David.

Marcella's eyes riveted to Diego's face, her hand snaking out to his arm, shackling it with anticipation. He started to get up, anger rolling through him like a part of the very air. She felt it in her mind. And in her body as if it breathed for her as well. "No," she said. "He's just trying to protect me."

David's angry voice bellowed again, the pounding getting louder. "Marcella."

"Just a minute," she called across the room, afraid David would wake the neighbors. It was a moment of distraction Diego took advantage of, pushing off the bed in a quick, agile move. Her hand fell away from his arm despite her best attempt to control him. Something raged within him, dark and dangerous.

"Diego," she said, a plea in her voice. He stood above her, ready to charge the door, naked as the day he was born.

The broad muscles of his chest expanded as he sucked in a deep breath. "This is between me and this man." A muscle in his jaw jumped. "You go into the bathroom."

"What?" she gasped, lifting her body onto her knees. "If you think for one minute—"

"Marcella," David called through the door. She frowned. Now she was hot. At both of these two fools. "Shut up and wait, David!" she yelled at the door, and then refocused on Diego. "You better get one thing straight, mister. I'm not some wimpy woman you can boss around."

Diego stared at her, not moving, his eyes locked with hers in silent challenge. "And I'm not sharing my woman."

"*Your* woman?" she demanded. "Is that what I am?"

"You wear my mark."

"I don't know anything about a mark. But if I am your woman—and right now the way you're acting—it's if," she warned, "then you need to believe in me." She paused and then softened her voice. "Trust me. I don't want David, but I do appreciate him looking out for me and you should too!"

His lips tightened. "He has motives."

"David is an honorable man. He's never acted out of line with me. I'm getting dressed and answering the door. I am begging you to stand by my side and support me. You've asked for a lot of trust from me. I need the same from you."

He reached for her hand. "I will always stand by you."

She looked up into his eyes and knew it was true. For reasons she still didn't fully comprehend, she belonged with him. "Prove it now. Get dressed and meet David. Treat him like the man who protected me until the day we came together, you and I."

"Answer one thing first."

"All right," she whispered.

"Are you my woman?"

"You know the answer."

His mouth came close to hers. "Say it."

"Yes," she said a bit breathlessly as his mouth closed down on hers.

* * * * *

Diego stood next to Marcella as she opened the hotel door. He reminded himself of the need for control. The possessiveness he felt for Marcella was new, his way of dealing with it far from defined.

David looked from one to the other, and then his eyes locked and focused on Marcella. Anticipating his move, Diego's hand shackled his wrist, as it was about to claim Marcella's arm. "Don't touch her," he warned and then released his grip.

David's eyes flashed with anger. "Marcella, you need to come with me."

"Come inside," Marcella said, taking Diego's arm and stepping backwards. "There is much we need to discuss." David didn't move.

"You don't even know this man," he argued.

"I do," she said, and responding to the doubt so evident in his eyes. "I do."

"Please," she added.

He stared at her a long moment and then let out a breath, taking a reluctant step forward. Diego was surprised when David's eyes locked with his, a challenge in his hard stare. Diego watched him walk several steps into the room and turn to face them. Marcella shut the door and then laced her arm under Diego's elbow. It was a clear message to David showing her commitment to Diego. This didn't displease him. But he also knew she did it for another reason.

A desire to keep him in check.

"How do you know him?" David asked.

A muscle jumped in his jaw. "My name is Diego Montez, not *him*."

David's brow lifted. "Okay, *Diego*," he said, a sharpness to the way he said the name. "How do you know Marcella?"

"David," Marcella said. "Diego is like me. He's different. We are connected in ways I can't explain."

David shook his head. "Tell me you aren't serious?"

"Marcella will be traveling to my home with me. Your services are no longer needed."

"Oh no," David said, and he stepped forward, moving towards Marcella.

"No, David!" Marcella yelled, and her hand went out in front of her, stop-sign fashion.

David's fist went to his chest, stopping as if he'd hit a brick wall. "What?" His eyes were wide. He took a step backward, a hint of desperation in his face. After several seconds his hand slipped to his side. Fixing Marcella in a stare, both his expression and his voice held accusation. "What did you just do?"

"I...I don't know." Marcella's face registered shock. "I didn't want you two to fight." She looked up at Diego and her hand went to her neck. "I didn't even know I could do that."

Diego turned to her, pulling her close. "It's okay. You meant only to protect him. I thought this might happen. All the power you possess is now enhanced. You are joined with me. My power is yours and yours is mine."

"This is crazy," David said, his voice full of force, but he didn't move. "What the hell have you done to her?"

"Enhanced?" Marcella echoed.

Diego ran his hands up and down her arms. "Yes. My power is yours."

"And mine is yours?" she asked.

"Together we are stronger."

David was growing impatient. "What the hell is going on?"

Marcella looked at him. "David, I think we should sit down and talk. Let Diego explain. I can't tell you what I have yet to figure out myself."

The phone rang. No one moved. Marcella felt Diego's tension level rise. It was like being plugged into his emotional outlet. Marcella looked at David. "It's my aunt."

"How do you know that?" he asked.

The phone continued to ring. She didn't often allow David to see just how perceptive she was, fearful that it would be unsettling for him. Besides, sometimes she was and sometimes she wasn't. She seemed to get feelings about things only when some deep part of her mind told her it was important. Granted, knowing someone was on the phone wasn't in her normal skill set. Still…"You know how I know. Can I get it without you starting trouble?"

David's face twisted. "I'll get it," he said, and sidestepped Marcella, about to pass her, when the phone went silent. He mumbled a curse and his eyes went to Diego's. "What have you done to her? Something is different."

* * * * *

Staring at David, Diego fought the urge to pick him up and force him from the room. But deep down, he felt the man's true concern for Marcella. For this reason alone, he forced civility.

"Marcella is safer with me than she has ever been. I will die for her if necessary. Of this, you have my word." Diego pulled Marcella under his arm, close to his side. "It will be her choice what she tells you. Leave us now. Go comfort her aunt. Tell her we will come to her soon and explain."

David looked at Marcella. "This is what you want?"

"Yes," she said. "Please don't frighten my aunt. Please tell her I'm safe." Marcella paused. "Because I am."

"This is what you really want?" David asked, fists balled at his sides. "You trust him over me." Not a question. A stark, cold fact.

"David," Marcella said in a soft voice. "There are things going on beyond the surface. Things I can't explain but I will."

His jaw tensed. "Explain now."

She took a deep breath and looked up at Diego. "Please give me a minute with him."

His first instinct was to say no, but the plea in her voice was impossible to ignore. He took a deep breath and looked at David. It wasn't outside of the man's range to think he might grab her and run. Diego gave him a warning look. Hard eyes met hard eyes.

Marcella squeezed his arm and he gave her his attention. Their eyes locked, and he spoke to her in his mind. *I will step to the window but I will not leave you alone. He is contemplating doing something stupid like grabbing you and making a run for it. I see it in his eyes.*

Her eyes went to David, lingered and then returned to Diego. *He is worried.*

Diego ground his teeth together. *Make him go away or I will.*

He's just trying to help.

Marcella —

Fine! I will handle him.

He eyed her a moment, making sure she meant her words, and then turned away. And then he positioned himself across the room, by the window, and watched. Prepared to act.

* * * * *

Marcella gave David her full attention, moving close to him and making eye contact. "I'm safe."

David rejected her answer. "He's a stranger. How do you know he's not dangerous?"

There was truth to his words and in the back of her mind she wondered at Diego's powers. Could he make her enthralled with mind tricks? Should she trust him? Everything inside screamed yes. But was it a trick she didn't understand? Well, one thing for sure. Diego didn't mean to harm her. She didn't think he could hide such a thing with her abilities. But his motives for wanting her…that might be a different story.

"Oh, I know he's dangerous," she admitted. "Just not to me." She paused and then spoke the remainder of what she knew to be truth. "But there *are* monsters after me. Diego can protect me."

David's face filled with frustration. "There are always monsters after you. That's why you hired me. And that's why I can't let you simply trust this guy."

"I do not simply trust a stranger. Give me some credit. He's different." She hesitated, holding back the words, *like me*. It felt the natural thing to say, but it wasn't true. It couldn't be. No one was like her. "Not…like you. And neither are the men after me." She paused again, considering. "David, they aren't wholly human. They…are just not. Diego. Well, the truth is, he's different as well."

His eyes went to Diego and then back to her. "What does that mean?"

"It means I know him in ways you can't comprehend. I am safe with him. Please leave me here tonight. I will explain more tomorrow."

He barely let her finish her final word, discarding the idea. "Forget it, Marcella. The more you talk, the more concerned I get."

She didn't know how to get him to understand. "David, if you don't leave…"

"What?" David challenged. His voice lifted. "He'll beat the crap out of me?"

"David—"

He looked at Diego. "Let him try."

Chapter Six

ॐ

Diego considered David a long moment. There was no doubt this man wanted his woman. Yet he also cared for her. He reached for his mind, pushing aside his jealousy with effort. And he found what he wanted. Honor. Trust. A willingness to die for Marcella. Things he had no option but to respect. The problem was he was also creating doubt in her. Something he didn't like nor could he afford. This coupled with his desire to please his mate played heavily in his soul. An emotional response that conflicted with the wilder, darker response that came more naturally. The one that wanted to beat the shit out of anyone who thought of Marcella in a physical way.

Yet he knew she was his. And with that knowledge he reached for his human side and shoved down the possessive need to lash out. He walked towards David and Marcella started towards him. Standing in front of him, her small frame meant to still him, her hands went to his chest.

"Please don't," she said hoarsely.

He reached for her and eased her against his body. David started forward, and Diego held up a staying hand and then he reached for his mind. He had the ability to influence human thought though it was a new skill he'd only recently allowed himself to utilize.

"Stop," Diego said firmly, a mental push behind the word. "I have something to show you."

David stilled, his eyes narrowing. Diego held his gaze, making sure he had accepted the command. GTECHS could present mental commands but some responded better than others. And eye contact was necessary while issuing the order. It was one of the skills used by the Arions to lure humans into their dangerous game of world domination. A mind push. A promise of power, wealth and physical perfection. But he'd been in their lair. He knew the ultimate goal. Those who didn't follow would be killed. The Arions planned to control humanity and then beyond.

Diego's hand went to Marcella's hair, and he lifted it, exposing her neck. David's eyes went wide. "What the hell is that?"

"What is what?" Marcella asked, reaching for her neck.

"My mark, Marcella. I'm making sure he knows you belong to me."

Her eyes locked with his. "Diego, I don't—"

"What?" David said. "Your mark? What in God's name is going on?"

"I want to see," Marcella said and then shrugged out of his hold. He released her immediately. Of course, she wanted to see.

And she should. As she scurried to the bathroom, Diego and David stood eye to eye. "She is my woman."

"Only if she chooses to be."

"She already has."

"Who the hell do you think you are?" David said. "No." A muscle in his jaw jumped. "*What* are you and what do you want with Marcella?"

"One of the good guys. There's a silent war raging. Man against beast. I'm one of the men who plan to save humanity. How about you?"

"Save humanity," he said, repeating the words. "And you're one of the good guys." He sounded like that was hard to believe. "If that's true, who are you fighting?"

"A group of soldiers called Arions. They are men enhanced with DNA samples from Area 51. Super Soldiers injected with alien DNA made to be stronger and more powerful than anything you could ever imagine. And some of them feel they are now the perfect race. The humans that don't follow will be condemned to die."

David laughed. "You don't really expect me to buy this, do you?"

"Believe what you want, but it won't change the facts."

Crossing his arms in front of his chest, David stood there a long moment. "Why should I believe you?"

"You know I'm different. I was injected as well, but like many others I chose to stay loyal to what I am to the core...human. I have become a Guardian of humanity rather than a destroyer. But I can't change what I am. I'm changed. And Marcella is my mate."

"What does Marcella have to do with you or any of this?"

"Only certain genetic lines are compatible with our males. Why that is we don't know. And even then, the compatible women only match one man. Again, we don't know why." He paused and then added, "Yet. We are trying to figure it out. But as it stands, there is only one woman who is my exact match. And that woman is Marcella."

David's face had taken on a shallow, ghostly look despite the warm brown of his skin tone. "And she accepts this as truth?"

Diego knew Marcella stood by the doorway to the bathroom and that she listened. And now seemed as good a time as any to explain the realities of their situation. "I am a doctor who has studied the new race with great depth. Mates know each other instantly. The connection is automatic. This was a surprise to me as well. I came here not to claim Marcella as my woman but to ask for her help. I had no idea she was my destiny."

David looked towards Marcella. Diego didn't. He felt what she did. She understood. As he had spoken she had reached in his mind and compared his words to the images he offered.

"So that mark on her neck means exactly what? Explain."

Diego smiled. "It matches the one on mine. It links us together. We are one."

They stood there in silence, David's eyes turbulent as he digested and slowly accepted. "Show me," Marcella said, breaking the silence.

* * * * *

A few moments later, Marcella found herself back to the bathroom mirror as Diego placed a small mirror in her hand while David stood in the doorway looking like he was chewing aspirin. Her stomach fluttered as she tried to shove her hair aside. Diego reached forward and helped her. He was so close and smelled so alluring and perfect. And knowing the implications of what she was being shown only seemed to make his allure more powerful. She wanted him. Again. It was crazy but so real and alive with heat she hardly knew how to reel it in. Her teeth found her bottom lip as she blinked and tried to focus.

Diego's fingers caressed her neck and then his eyes went to hers. She focused on what she saw in the mirror. A star. It was etched in her skin, bigger than a quarter. More like two. And though she had limited vision, the perfection of every corner seemed near impossible. It wasn't a human design.

Suddenly, David moved, stepping closer and leaning towards her. "It's a tattoo, Marcella. It has to be." He touched it and looked at Diego. "Did you drug her?" Then to Marcella, "Do you remember falling asleep at any point this evening?"

Diego was on edge, and Marcella knew it. David was way too close to him and far too loaded with attitude. He had no idea how much he was pushing his luck. And worse, he was pushing her. Why couldn't he trust her? He knew damn well she was unique. For her to have strange things happen wasn't unusual.

She set the mirror down and moved her head so Diego would drop her hair. "Oh, good grief, David. Don't be so accusing."

He stared at her with disbelief in his eyes. His gaze lifted and locked with Diego's. "You believe him over me?" Then to Diego, "What did you do to her?"

Marcella lifted her hand and grabbed Diego's wrist, feeling the anger inside him like a crossfire she'd been caught in. *Don't.*

Diego's face didn't change, but he spoke to her with irritation evident in his voice. *I'm losing patience with him.*

She focused on David. "I need you to trust me, David. I'm not in danger." She paused. "At least not from Diego."

David's chest rose and fell with heavy breaths. His eyes moved from Diego to Marcella. "You choose this path?"

"Path?" she asked, not certain what he meant.

His voice was low but intense. "I cannot control what happens to you if you turn your back on my protection."

Diego answered. "Her choice was made long ago. I am her destiny. And I am her protector."

David's gaze stayed on Marcella. "Decide, Marcella."

"Don't do this—"

He took a step backwards. "You're being foolish. Think about what this means. I will be close." A pause. "For now. Once you leave this hotel without me, there is no turning back."

She watched as David pivoted on his heels and left the room. A moment of uncertainty kept her from moving. But then she knew she had to follow. She took off walking. He'd been good to her, and she hated how this was ending. "David—"

But her words were cut off by the door slamming. She rushed forward determined to follow, but Diego's words stilled her. "No. It's dangerous."

She swallowed. A part of her was relieved David was gone. The entire time he had been in the room with Diego she'd felt as if she was holding back two bulls about to charge.

The battle cries, though only in their minds, had been potent with life. She flipped the locks shut, her instincts telling her Diego was right. Someone hunted her. She turned and rested against the wooden surface, watching Diego watch her. Something dark was beneath his surface. As sure as she drew another breath, she knew her long-term bodyguard had her best interest at heart.

The star. The way she felt with Diego. It was true she wasn't the same. Diego had changed her. Perhaps forever. "What *did* you do to me?"

He didn't immediately answer. "Are you afraid?"

Her eyes narrowed. "You know I'm not." She paused. "But I should be."

His brow inched upward, and he stepped towards her. "Why?" he asked. "Because logic says you should be?" With each word he took a step. "Or because normal humans fear the unknown?"

She watched him close the distance between them, feeling the pulse of anticipation beneath her skin. Wanting answers to questions she didn't even understand. It was confusing. He tied her in knots. "Exactly."

"But you're *not* normal," he said. "Never have been nor will you ever be again."

"Not by human standards, I'm not. But by my own neither are you." Even as she spoke the words, Marcella knew they didn't ring true. He had changed her.

"You are very much like me." Diego stood in front of her now and extended his hand. "Come," he said. "I'll teach you all you want to know."

She looked down at his hand. For a split second Marcella tried to resist the lure he held. But it was a useless endeavor. Going to him was like running to the warmth of a flame on a cold day. Impossible to resist.

But as she slipped her hand in his, she willed herself to remain strong. She would only give him a piece of her.

He was, after all, a stranger with an agenda she couldn't begin to understand.

Or could she?

* * * * *

David stepped outside the hotel, frustration deep in his soul. The area was deserted, the lights low and the night dark. His strides were long as he walked with a hurried pace. He needed air and space. The way Marcella had clung to the stranger's side had him in knots. It twisted and burned like acid in an open wound.

He'd always felt things for Marcella. Things he shouldn't. After all, he was her protector. Getting personal complicated things. But somewhere along the line, it had happened. He had fallen in love with Marcella.

The woods were heavy to his left. The solitude they offered called to him with a strange magnetic pull. It was unlike him to retreat but for some reason it felt compelling. Even necessary. Though there was no one around, he didn't like the prospect. His mind raced with turbulent thoughts. This new stranger represented trouble and he knew it. His sudden appearance alone would have been suspicious, but the way Marcella responded to him was simply crazy. He was a stranger. Had the man cast some sort of spell on her?

He was now past the main scenery of the hotel, brush crunching beneath his boots. Running actually crossed his mind. Anything that might let off the steam burning beneath his skin. Yet he held back, knowing he couldn't stray too far. What if Marcella needed him? Yet emotions clogged his mind and made a clear plan difficult to conceive. Every instinct he owned pressed him to go back after Marcella.

He stopped walking, though he really wanted to keep moving, knowing he needed to stay near the hotel. Even now, he should return. But he needed just a minute more. With a deep breath, he took a seat on a large rock. And that's when he noticed it…the total, complete silence.

Not one branch moved. Not one leaf fluttered. A slow awareness slid down his spine as evil as a snake slivering to its prey. And he knew, without a doubt, he was being watched. *Damn it!* Had he been lured from Marcella? What insanity had possessed him to walk into the woods?

Careful not to make any rash moves, he forced himself to remain still. Discreetly, he eyed the left and then the right. But still nothing. Not a single movement. It was almost…unearthly.

A sudden gush of wind tore through the air and he dug his palms against the hard stone. Everything calm became chaos. Tree limbs ripped from the root, leaves flew through the air. And then as if out of nowhere, two men approached. No. They were more beast than men. Their hair was long, flowing in the wind behind their broad shoulders. Snarls painted their faces with anger, challenging looks no doubt meant to intimidate.

David pushed to his feet and stood, stance wide, hand sliding to his waist, resting on his gun. He didn't dare draw it, but the comfort of knowing it was near held a calming impact. Facing his opponents, he was prepared to act. He might be outnumbered but he wasn't weak or afraid. The bigger of the two challengers sported a deep gash on his face. He stepped forward taking the lead. He took a step as well, showing these men—or whatever the hell they were— he was up for the challenge.

The aggressive one spoke. "You have two options on this night."

David's brow lifted. "Let me guess...live or die." He paused for effect. "Not very original."

"Actually, death is one very real option."

A scraping noise drew David's attention to the man's hands. Blades were extending from his skin. What the hell? His heart beat faster as he tried to process what must be an illusion. He blinked. Shit. It seemed real. Like blades really came from his skin. His mind flashed back to Marcella's words. Monsters she had called her new enemies.

And he knew in that moment that Diego was not the bad guy. He was indeed just the opposite. He'd allowed jealousy to taint his usual instinct. Making eye contact with his enemy, he stiffened his spine.

He focused on coming off strong. A gun would surely kill these things. "Death is an option, no doubt. For you and me."

The monster smiled as did his companion. "You are no match for me and neither is the gun you hope will save you."

David felt as if the breath was knocked out of his chest. How could he know his thoughts? He swallowed. Marcella had abilities. Could these things have powers even greater than hers? Reaching deep for calm, he rationalized. It could be a logical guess. An intimidation tactic.

"Right. You're bulletproof."

Laughter followed. The creature held out his arms. "Care to try me?"

No. That was what came to mind. Somehow he didn't think this was going well. "I don't play games. What do you want?"

"It's what you want. I can give you power, skill and the woman of your dreams. Do I have your attention?"

He didn't want to know what this guy was talking about. It wasn't good, he knew that much, and it was enough. "Whatever you are getting at, forget it."

The shorter of the two stepped forward, and razors shot from his hands. "I'm afraid we can't do that."

Suddenly, David felt a force in his mind. Like a low hum. Pressure. He squeezed his eyes shut against the pain.

"Stop fighting and the pain will end." The voice felt distant yet close. In his head. He pressed his palms over his ears. Somehow he had to fight. He had to warn Marcella. In his mind, he cried out as he fell to his knees.

* * * * *

Marcella felt the weight of Diego like a heavy, seductive blanket of fulfillment. He shuddered with release. Hers had come only moments before, drawing from her a sigh of utter satisfaction. There had been no time to ask questions or even think them. The minute they had touched passion had flared. One minute she stood at the door of the room, the next she was naked, beneath him, in total bliss. After several moments of simply clinging together, sated and pressed close, Diego rolled over and pulled her to his shoulder. His hand stroked her hair with tender, gentle caresses.

But suddenly the peace of the moment was gone. Her mind raged with a fierce cry. Squeezing her eyes shut, she tried to understand what was happening. A sharp pain knifed into her stomach. She sat up, holding her middle.

"David," she gasped.

Diego was already sitting, having followed her movement, his hands on her arms. "I know, my love," he said. "I'm going to him."

She turned, blinking Diego into focus. "Hurry. He's hurt."

Already standing, he reached for his clothes. "I'm going," he said. "Lock the door and don't open it until I say so. And I mean not for anyone but me."

Feeling the reality of the present rather than the distant fog of her vision, Marcella scrambled to the side of the bed. "No," she said, "I have to go. What if he needs to be healed?"

"Forget it." Diego's voice was firm. "You're not going anywhere." He reached for his shirt and tugged it over his head.

Marcella grabbed her skirt from the floor and stepped into it. "What if he's hurt? You might need me."

Marcella, I'm a doctor. I can handle David's injuries. I don't want you getting hurt in the process."

She reached for her blouse, not bothering with a bra. There wasn't time. No way could she stay here and bear the anguish of waiting. "I'm going. I have the ability to fight. You saw what I did to David."

"David is nothing compared to these men."

She reached for her shoes. "I'm going, Diego. If you leave me I will follow."

* * * * *

She'd left him no real option. On the other hand, Diego knew the dangerous ground he was treading on. There was no time for debate, so he went with his gut instincts. The minute he took a step towards her, she backed up, clearly reading his intent. Perhaps even his mind. She had the ability to and he did nothing to block his mind. Marcella was his mate. It was his duty to protect her.

"You wouldn't," she said, a tightness to her voice that said she knew he indeed would.

"You leave me no option, woman."

She took another step. So did he. "Diego, stop!" There was no time. He took two long strides and tossed her as gently as possible over his shoulder. "Oh my God," she said. "No! You aren't doing this. The blood is running to my head, damn it! Put me down, you beast!"

He grabbed the ties off the curtains. Beast. Yes, he was. Their leader, Mason, had always feared the more primal part of who he was. Diego wasn't. He was confident in the human side of his being. And he knew it controlled the darker part of his being. "I am that and more, Marcella. Don't test me."

The bed had a padded board and nothing to tie her to. He sat her on the floor and formed a V over her body with his, easily trapping her. He pulled her hands in front of her body and wrapped them. All the while she complained and called him names.

Her hands now bound, she fumed. "I won't forgive you for this."

He gave her a hard stare. She squirmed. He needed to attach her to the bed. "The longer it takes me to complete this task the longer David goes without help. A minute could cost him his life."

And those words calmed her. She stilled. "I can't believe you're doing this."

"You forced my actions." He looped the other tie around the bed frame but now he needed to connect it to the one around her wrists. "The only way I can be certain you don't get away is if your hands go above your head."

Her eyes went wise. "Please," she whispered. "Diego, don't do this."

He moved her, not waiting for her agreement, his body still over hers. With her flat on her back, he pushed her hands over her head. And then he brushed his lips over hers. "You leave me no option." He secured her, leaving no slack. "I'll be back soon."

Without another moment's pause, he headed to the door. David was being tortured. The Arions were trying to force him to go to their side. And he was resisting.

Which made him a man worth saving.

Chapter Seven

ဆ

Diego walked through the lobby of the hotel with a cool exterior but he felt the heat of urgency. And David's pain played on his nerve endings like a low hum. Something he'd experienced in the past with others, but only when he made an effort to reach for a mind. David's pain seemed to call to him automatically. It was a unique sensation he expected came from his connection to Marcella. He was quickly realizing their combined powers had created an evolution of sorts. Not only did she have many of his powers, she had her own. The way she had stopped David with her mind had been a shock. He had this ability but it was practiced. She had done it effortlessly. They had hoped her powers would allow her to develop the skills of others. He had no doubt now. She had much to offer.

The moment he was in the coverage of the woods, he disappeared into the wind and reappeared only a foot away from David. Both Arions snarled at him and Diego faced them, ready to fight. But with his mind, he reached for David, feeling his pain and creating a buffer to ease the intensity. Though he'd resisted working his mind powers in manipulative ways, he'd mastered the art of blocking pain.

The bigger of the two Arions hovered near David. "I thought you were here to see Grandma?"

He ignored his taunting question. "Don't you have anything better to do than terrorize humans?"

"I suppose you're here to stop us," the shorter one said.

"Smart guy," Diego said.

"But you're not or you wouldn't have changed sides."

The other Arion added, "Or come here alone." Diego extended the razors from his wrists in silent challenge. The two Arions started towards him. Diego's time spent studying the Arions gave him an upper hand. He knew the weak spots of his enemy. With that came confidence. It didn't change the fact he was outnumbered, but he had to survive for the sake of Marcella.

"Need help?"

Diego knew the voice to his left. Michael. His mind drew a picture, but his eyes remained on his enemy. Well over six feet tall, with massive arms and black hair that hung like a lion's mane to his shoulders, Michael was potent in battle. And a nice surprise right about now. The Knights called him the Guardian Angel. Michael claimed all Knights as the Guardians of humanity. It had been Michael who had led the Knights caught in the Arion circle in an uprising. And it had been Michael who had helped the Knights' leaders assume his power and accept the battle to come.

Diego focused on the bigger of the Arions who was now pacing from left to right in front of him, but he spoke to Michael. "Never did like to miss a battle, did you, Michael?"

"Mason didn't like the idea of you out here alone."

Diego didn't reply. He saw the flash of metal as the Arion drove his sharp blade at him. Diego caught it with his own and then thrust his other arm forward only to find it blocked. He'd angered his enemy, making him curse under his breath.

Diego lifted a brow. "Not as easy to beat as you expected, I take it?"

The Arion made a frustrated sound and ground his feet deeper into the dirt. He and Diego pressed against each other, blade to blade, each forcing the other forward and then backwards. Finally, they shoved off each other. Diego and the Arion ended up bouncing backwards several steps.

Out of the corner of his eye, Diego saw the other Arion move behind him. In front of him, Diego's adversary disappeared into the wind. Damn it, he hated...that shit.

Standing above David an Arion held a knife. His eyes locked with Diego's. "I should just kill your man and be done with him," the Arion said. The threat proved worthless when Michael appeared behind the Arion and shoved a knife directly into the enemy's heart, killing him.

A quick sweep for the second Arion and Diego found him dead at Michael's hand. Diego gave Michael a quick nod. "You made my job easy."

Michael smiled. "Looks to me like you need your energy to play healer," he said, inclining his head towards David.

And then he heard Marcella in his head. *Bring him to me.* He hadn't expected her to be able to reach to him from such a distance.

I'm on my way.

* * * * *

100

Marcella heard the door open. She had mixed feelings about her current position. She was hot about being tied to the bed, but not as much as she had been a few minutes before. She'd felt Diego's battle in her mind. And she knew he had protected David. A part of her knew he'd done it for her as well.

For now, she knew to put aside the whirlwind of confusion she felt. For now, she needed to help tend to David. But later she had things to say to Diego. Groundwork and boundaries to be set. She wasn't going to be a pawn to his orders.

"Diego?" she called out. Even though she knew it was him entering the room, she needed to hear his voice.

"Yes," he said, "I'm here." He squatted beside her, releasing her ties.

The sound gave her a rush of relief beyond what was normal. She hardly knew this man yet she feared for him as if he was her family. She rubbed her wrists and sat up, concerned. "Where is he?"

He started to move away and she knew he felt a rush of some sort. But she reached for his arm, needing his touch for some reason she didn't quite process. It simply was what it was. Real and urgent. When she should be smacking his face for tying her up, she was compelled to connect with him. She hated her own lack of reason. And touching him seemed to connect her to what he was feeling. The mental path they shared expanded.

And with that one contact, she confirmed what she already knew... "It's bad, isn't it?"

Averting his gaze, he seemed to want to shield her from the truth. But she already knew. "It's not good." He pushed to his feet and offered her his hand. There was urgency to his actions. "Hold the door and I'll bring him in. I need to get him out of sight fast."

She swallowed and slid her hand in his. Pushing to her feet. The minute she was steady, he moved towards the door. Not giving herself time to stretch her stiff limbs, she pressed forward and reached for the door. She'd barely pulled it open when Diego stepped through the doorway. He had David in his arms and rushed passed her. And to her surprise, so did another man. Big, with long raven hair, the stranger followed Diego to the bed.

Marcella shut the door and locked it. Something about securing them inside felt necessary. Whoever this newcomer was, he was a friend to Diego. She wasn't sure what that made him to her. Everything was too crazy. Too out of control. She really wanted to understand what was happening to her. To step back and analyze and meditate. But there was no time.

Diego was already leaning over David and she needed to focus on what was needed of her as a healer. She went to the opposite side of the bed and glanced at the stranger. He handed Diego several towels and then fixed Marcella in a look. "Michael, ma'am," he said, answering her unasked question. "And I know when to stand back and let the experts do their thing." With that said he stepped away.

Whoever he was he seemed to respect how odd his presence was to her. And he seemed to know she needed to feel some semblance of comfort to heal. He knew of her powers. How she didn't know but he knew. She watched him take a position in the far corner near a window. He turned to face them. She stood watching for an instant and then turned her attention to David. With a little more of a comfort level for the people in the room, she could now focus.

"His pulse is low," Diego said, pressing a towel to the wound that ran from one side of his chest to the other. He'd ripped the front of David's shirt at some point, clearing the injury for examination. All Marcella could see was blood and tissue. It was a deep, dangerous wound.

She could heal, but from the inside out. She couldn't stop bleeding. What she did was different than what David needed at this very moment. "He has to go to a hospital."

Diego shook his head. "We can't do that. We have limited time. More Arions will come for him…" Their eyes locked. "And us."

"He's bleeding way too much though." She felt David's weakness. He wasn't in good shape. He played on her mind in a low hum rather than the loud rumble of his usual presence.

Diego lifted the towel and studied the cut. Marcella stared at the deep tear in the flesh. "What did they cut him with?"

For a moment, Diego looked as if he didn't want to answer. His gaze focused on David and the wound. "Arions have razor extensions from their wrists. Like fish fins but a hundred times sharper." He glanced at her and she knew her face registered her shock. Did Diego, the man she had been intimate with, also have these…things in his body? What were these men?

"I could stitch him," Diego said, but his voice held doubt.

"But?" she asked, sensing his hesitation, trying to forget about the implications of what she had just learned.

David murmured and tossed his head. Diego frowned. "That is exactly my concern. He's too alert. I have nothing for pain. I don't know the extent of his internal injuries but I expect they are quite severe. The pain could send him into cardiac arrest. I think we need to clean him up and bandage him."

"Won't he need antibiotics?" Michael asked from across the room. "Sterling's on his way. Is there somewhere he can pick some up?"

"Yes," Diego said, but he didn't look at David. "I know someone."

Diego was staring at the wound. And Marcella could see the debate in his eyes. His eyes lifted to Marcella's. "Let's start with taping him up nice and tight. In the closet there's a small black suitcase. You should find bandages and some antiseptic."

She nodded, more than eager to help in any way possible. It didn't surprise her he didn't ask if she could heal David. Diego seemed to know her in ways that still surprised her. She retrieved the items he requested and then watched as he poured the medicine on David's chest. Then she stepped backwards to allow Michael to assist. The two men lifted David and wrapped him tight before taping him.

Once the task was complete, Diego made several phone calls. "The antibiotics will be here in a couple of hours. Now all we can do is wait." He paused. "Unless there is something you can do for him."

She bit her bottom lip. Healing more than one person in a small window of time wasn't something she had ever done. Just healing one person drained her completely. If

Diego managed to control the bleeding, David would still need help. If she helped him, the little girl might suffer.

Marcella felt the weight of Diego's eyes. "What is it, Marcella?"

She looked up at him. "I fear I have to choose David's life or the little girl's."

Chapter Eight

Diego wanted to help Marcella through the obvious distress she felt. He closed the distance between them and pulled her close, hating the news he had to deliver. She could heal David but not the child. "*Mi amor*, we cannot stay until morning. It is too dangerous."

She stiffened. "What?" The words came out choked. "I have to stay. That little girl needs me."

"He is right," Michael said. "It is far too dangerous."

"No." It was an immediate, sharp response. "I *have* to be here for this family. I promised." She tried to pull away from Diego, but he held her. "Let go." She spoke through clenched teeth. "You can't make me leave. You keep trying to make me do things I don't want to. This is my life. My way. Everything is out of control and I'm not taking it anymore. Stop doing this to me!"

"I'm not doing this, Marcella. Not to you. Not to David. And not to that little girl." He paused long enough to let his words sink in. "They are. The Arions have motives we can't control. If you die what good will it serve? Think how many children might not be helped. Think how many children might lose their parents to these monsters."

Her breathing was heavy now. "How do I know you aren't one of those monsters?"

It hurt to have her question him, but he knew she was confused. He stroked her hair, relieved when she didn't fight him. She was his mate, and his touch would offer comfort even if she didn't understand her reaction. Slowly, she eased into him. His heart twisted with emotion. "I wish this wasn't as it is. I wish I could change how we met."

She grabbed the front of his shirt, clutching at him as if she needed support. And he felt her mind peak with a rush of wild thoughts. Fears. Pain. "I can't leave that little girl to die."

"There simply is no option," Michael said firmly, drawing both their attention. "Marcella," he explained, "those Arions that damaged David came for *you*. He was punished because he refused to betray you."

She sucked in a breath and Diego ran his hands up and down her arms. Michael meant well. He was giving her a needed jolt of reality but it didn't ease the heaviness of the words. "I know," she whispered. Then in a louder voice, "I could feel his resistance. I knew he was protecting me."

Michael looked at her with his hard, emotionless eyes. The ones he used in times of war. But they weren't an indication of who he was. Diego knew the honor and the heart that was Michael.

"I know this is hard," Michael said, "but we must change hotels. The Marquee has basement-level rooms."

"What does that have to do with anything?" Marcella said, confusion in her voice. Her tone lifted slightly, almost insistently. "The girl is coming here."

Diego looked her with a direct stare. When he told her things he knew sounded hard to swallow, he wanted to her to see the truth in either his eyes or his mind. "Underground the Arions can't track us. Just as you can sense things in people, they can as well. If they get a read on you, they can find you. It's like a dog getting a scent. We aren't safe here."

"Even a hotel move is risky," Michael said. "We need to leave the minute our backup gets here."

Diego didn't look at Michael because he knew he wasn't going to like what he was about to say. "We move and then tomorrow morning we can bring the girl to you." He paused, feeling the disapproval of Michael like a charge across the room. "And then we leave."

She swallowed. "I don't understand any of this. And...so we can stay for the child?"

"It's foolish," Michael said.

Diego hesitated. Michael was his superior. If he insisted on leaving he'd have to agree. But Michael said no more. Diego owed him a thank you. One thing was certain, Michael believed GTECHS were better off with mates. He believed it tamed them and kept them from their more animalistic impulses. If Michael felt leaving without taking care of the child would injure his bond with Marcella, he would give it consideration. Even more so, Michael knew Marcella might help their cause. To have her loyalty was important.

Finally Diego said, "We have to stay."

Marcella's hand went to his face. A silent thanks. "I still have to choose between the child and David. And I don't want to leave."

Michael started for the door. "I'll step out of the room and arrange the other hotel." His tone was clipped and tight with irritation. He might support Diego's decision but he was going to give him hell about it.

The minute they were alone, he bent at the knees to look her in the eyes. "We have to get out of here. It's a must. The sooner the better."

She shook her head, rejecting his words. "We can't move David. He won't make it and if I heal him I'm not sure I can heal the girl. If he can make it until I heal her then—"

He cut her off. "There are options," he said. "The problem is, I don't know our full power together, but I'm certain we have abilities we didn't before. You saw how you stopped David with your mind."

Her eyes lit a bit. "You mean we could combine our power and save David and the girl?"

"I can't promise."

A look of disappointment crossed her face. "We can't risk it then." She glanced at David. "Can he make it until tomorrow night? If I have several hours to rest after the girl I think it will be enough."

"There are things I can do to lessen his pain with my mind and keep him relaxed. This will help him heal."

She gave him a frustrated look. "You didn't answer my question."

He wanted to protect her but he also had to be honest. "I can only try my best."

A long moment passed. Her eyes probed his face, studying him with intense eyes. "Who are you, Diego?"

She'd asked this question the first time they'd met. He knew she was trying to understand their connection. "I am your mate. The man who will do anything to please you. The man who will protect you with my life. But you must trust me."

"You tied me up."

"I won't allow you to make decisions that will jeopardize your life."

"You don't own me."

She didn't understand. He knew it was hard. They had so little time and he needed her to accept. "You belong to me, Marcella."

Her chin lifted with defiance. "No one owns me."

Her rebellion was strong. This was not going to be easy. This wasn't about ownership. "I belong to you as well." He let his emotions flow in the words and reached for her mind without being invasive. Just mentally pressing the truth of what he felt out there where she could reach for it if she so desired.

She didn't respond immediately but her expression registered surprise at his words. Her voice softened. "What if I don't want you to?"

He stepped closer and slid his fingers into her hair. "Oh, but you do." His voice was hoarse because her nearness evoked such a rush of heat. She was like a drug he craved. Yearning burned deep in his soul. His cock was hard and his heart open. There were no words adequate enough to explain what he felt. He lowered his head and used touch to speak, brushing his lips against hers in a soft, sensual caress. She shivered in his arms, and he knew she was as lost as he was. Only she didn't accept. Not yet. "In time you will embrace what we are together."

She was leaning into him, and with each moment she seemed to sink closer. Melting into his body. "I...I don't understand any of this."

Diego felt her confusion and wished he could erase it. All he wanted to do was make love to her. And show her how powerful their joining truly was. But she needed rest and there was much to be dealt with. "It is a lot to absorb," he said gently. He used his finger to trace her bottom lip. "And one day you will. Just not this one. Soon you will see my home and my people. They are your people too now. You will be lifted into an amazing world of passion and bravery. This is bigger than you or me. This is about the world."

And she was his life. A part of his very soul.

* * * * *

Less than an hour later Marcella stood at her aunt's door with Diego by her side. She knocked because somewhere in all the craziness she'd lost her key. The door flew open, and her aunt's eyes went wide. She wore a gown of pale blue and a robe that matched. Her grayish black hair was pinned in a bun, the top was wild with stray hairs. As if she'd been fretting and touching it with nervous hands.

She grabbed Marcella and hugged her. "I've been so worried."

Marcella felt the warmth of her hands touch with a sense of the familiar. "I'm fine," she said, rubbing her back to offer comfort.

Catherine pulled back and looked at Diego. Her eyes narrowed with a question. And perhaps a hint of suspicion. "So you're the young man who has influenced my niece to run wild?"

Diego smiled. "She has done the same to me, I assure you." He motioned to the door. "Can we go inside? We really must talk and quickly."

Despite the urgency of his tone, Marcella was pleased with Diego's response to her aunt. He liked her. She felt it. They entered the room and Diego shut the door and locked it. Catherine placed her hands on her full hips and stared at him, her probing gaze reflecting her intellect. "Who exactly are you?"

"I am the man who is going to save your niece's life."

* * * * *

The wind lifted with a flutter of limbs on the trees. Three Arions appeared in the shadows. They stood there in complete, utter stillness, the wind gone as if it never existed. They watched the Knights escort the humans to a car.

One of them spoke to the leader. "Should we take them now?"

"No," Damion said. "The woman is the Healer's mate. She could bring him back to our side. We will wait until the opportune moment and take them prisoner."

The third Arion interjected. "Why not now?"

Damion turned to him, a hiss to his voice. His razor extended from his left hand, driven by anger. Stupidity never set well. "Do not question me. We wait."

Fool. If he let them rush the Knights without a plan, it would be suicide. That would leave him with no prize to take to his King. He knew the men with the Healer. Michael, Sterling and another called Marcus. Michael had once been the right-hand man for their King. These were some of the best men the Knights had in their army.

Damion was ready for his place in power. He would not act rashly and fail. He had a prize to take home. One he would be rewarded for. "Follow them."

* * * * *

Marcella was alone in a dark room in a different hotel. This whole underground thing bothered her. When Diego had explained the Arions' ability to track people, she had been dumbfounded. The implications were clear. Now she not only had to live her life in hiding but below the surface of the earth. No sunlight. No real world experiences. Maybe if she just found a far-off city in some off-the-wall location she would be okay. Clearly, she couldn't stay in Mexico, and that saddened her. She'd become used to it here. It felt like home.

Or as close to it as someone on the run all the time could get.

Diego, Michael and her aunt were in the adjoining room looking out for David. They all wanted her to rest. And to properly heal the child she needed to. But she lay in the king-size bed feeling restless and out of sorts despite her exhaustion. And she found herself longing for Diego in a way she had never longed for another. She so needed the comfort he offered. Though she feared the things around her, she had the courage to face what was to come. Still, her whole world felt foreign to her. Life as she had known it would never be the same. Though she led a rather secluded life, moving from small town to small town, she had learned to enjoy the safe zone she called her world.

Yet…Diego felt like home.

But since he'd come into her life everything was out of control. Was he her savior or the destroyer in angel clothing? And now, her protector of the past, her bodyguard, David lay in the next room near death. He'd been a good friend and he'd been loyal to her this day. And it might just cost him his life.

If Diego had never entered the picture would David be where he was now?

She pressed her eyes shut, willing herself to rest. Energy was important for her healing abilities to work. After several seconds, punching her pillow, she turned to her side. Why was this happening?

* * * * *

Diego stood staring down at David, concerned over his progress. Michael, and now Sterling and Catherine, also surrounded the bed. He sighed, feeling the need for food and rest. Diego had stitched his wound with supplies Sterling had brought, which included pain medication, but it wasn't enough. His internal injuries were extreme. "He's not good."

"Marcella can't help?" Michael asked.

Catherine shook her head. Her graying hair was tied in a knot at the back of her head, making the tension in her wrinkled features more evident. There was a quiver to her voice. "Healing completely drains her." She sat down on the bed and picked up David's hand and she had goodbye in her eyes. "She will never help the child if she helps him." A shaky breath escaped her throat. "Poor David. He really has been good to my Marcella."

Silence filled the room.

"There is an option," Sterling said, drawing everyone's attention.

Diego found this as no surprise. He knew what was about to be suggested. Sterling tended to tread on water others didn't. He was known as the Renegade because he often pressed into the unknown and risky. A tall man with a long, muscular body, he looked the role of a gladiator.

He had long blond hair like a lion's mane and blue eyes so brilliant they often drew attention.

Diego's eyes locked with Sterling's. "No," Diego said, rejecting the idea before it was spoken.

Sterling didn't back down. Not that Diego thought he would. "It will save his life. I see no other option."

"You know how I feel about this." Diego was a man with strong principles and he had often spoken against what was suggested. "He can't make the decision himself. You had a choice." And in the back of his mind, Diego felt guilt at taking Marcella's choices. He knew she would have picked him. Mates wanted to be together. But the way time had pressed him to push had been dangerous. He'd acted because it was best for her safety. Together they were stronger. But how did he earn her trust? Could he?

Sterling's voice brought him out of his reverie. "And I chose the advantage of transforming to survive in battle."

"But not on your death-bed," Diego argued. "You chose while alive and well and with full understanding of the implications."

And Diego knew he had made the mating choice for Marcella. He'd asked her to accept their connection but in the heat of the moment he knew he had influenced her response. Just by being there, touching her, he'd made her want him. But he would not completely convert her without her request. She was bonded to him now, yes. But her body was not converted to that of this new species.

"What are you two talking about?" Catherine asked. "Can you save him?"

Diego looked at her. "No one said he wasn't going to make it."

"But he will make it for sure if you do this my way," Sterling added.

"How?" Catherine asked.

"Nothing is certain," Diego countered. Promises about life and death were dangerous.

Michael sighed. "I'm afraid I have to side with Sterling." He spoke the words against Diego's wishes though it was obvious they came with heaviness. "If you want this man to survive, and I sense it is important to your mate, then you must convert him."

"Mate?" Catherine questioned, pushing to her feet. "Why did you call her his mate?"

Diego's lips thinned. "It's a long story, and Marcella is restless. I need to go to her."

"I need answers," Catherine insisted. "You can't just dismiss me like this."

Michael looked at Catherine. "Does David live or die? You must make the call."

Her mouth hung open. "How can I answer when I'm not sure what I'm being asked?"

Diego looked at her and he saw a distinctive woman with courage and pride and ripe beauty. An older Marcella. From the moment he'd met Catherine, she had been strong and fearless. She'd faced adversity with her chin high. And now she dared to question, even when it meant someone she cared about could die.

The room was silent, waiting for Diego's answer. It was now his call. He had to make a decision that shouldn't be his to make. And he knew he held this man's future in his hands. Marcella stirred in his mind, a soft whisper of concern. She wanted David to survive. She wanted the child to survive. And she expected him to find an answer. Perhaps it was even a silent test…was he to be trusted?

With this realization came a decision. He looked at Catherine. "We aren't like you. Or David. Or any human."

Her eyes went wide. Diego moved towards her, his fingers touching her elbow as he guided her to the small table in the corner. They sat down across from one another and he started explaining. It was several minutes later when he finished by saying, "So you see, David can survive, but he will never be the same."

She stiffened her spine as if a decision was forming. "But if you convert him he can fight these creatures in the future without this happening."

Diego wanted to make sure she looked at this both ways. She'd taken in the information with remarkable acceptance and calm. But then Catherine knew Marcella was different. She understood everything in the world wasn't as black and white as humanity wanted it to be. Hell, as he wished it was.

Diego urged her to consider the negatives. "He will be better equipped but there is no way to know what the long-term effects of our condition are."

"I want him to live. We need men like David in such a fight. We are not better off without him." She pushed to her feet. "How can I help?"

Diego wasn't sure if he felt relieved or more stressed. Her use of the word "we" surprised him. This woman who hardly knew them now considered herself a part of their world. He could only hope she would help Marcella join him as well. But right now, the need for nourishment was beating on his body, and thinking was getting difficult. As his body weakened so did his ability to focus.

The metabolic rate of calories for a GTECH was extreme. He glanced at David who was pasty looking and completely knocked out.

He hated transitioning him without his approval. But waiting could put him at risk. If they were attacked they wouldn't be able to save him and fight. Or even transport him. Diego stood. "If we could get his approval I will feel better."

Michael stepped forward, focused on Catherine. "This won't be a complete conversion. We can't finish the process until we get back to the lab. What we do here, today, will only allow him to heal and help him survive."

"Diego," Sterling said, breaking a lengthy silence. "You need to eat."

Diego glanced at him and nodded. "Yes, I know, but I want to get this done."

"Then use my blood," Sterling said. He walked to the dresser and pulled a bottle of orange juice from the ice bucket. "And drink this. You know you can't go without it."

Diego accepted the drink but rejected the idea. "You're too newly converted. I don't want to risk weakening your system."'

"Then use mine," Michael said.

"Blood?" Catherine said, a bit hoarsely.

"Yes," Diego said, "a transfusion will partially convert him. Our blood has unique healing properties." He walked to his medical bag and withdrew tape and bandage. He then went to David's side, directly across from Michael. He looked at Catherine. "You might want to turn your head. Without the comforts of a medical facility we are doing this the only way possible."

She stared at him and then said, "I'm fine. Continue."

Michael brought his wrist to his mouth and bit down. Catherine made a sound and then covered her mouth. Diego pulled David's mouth. Michael held his wrist over the man's lips.

"He'll choke," Catherine objected and stepped forward. Her voice raised a notch as she repeated her concern. "He'll choke. No!"

Sterling reached for her. "He won't."

She squirmed in his arms. "He will."

"Look," Sterling told her, pointing. David had starting lapping at the flood.

The adjoining door flew open and Marcella appeared dressed in a pair of sweatpants and t-shirt. With her hair ruffled and wild, to Diego she looked casual and sexy and good enough to be his dinner. But her expression was one of concern. "What's wrong?" Her eyes went to her aunt and then to David. "What is he doing? What..." Her words broke off as if she didn't know quite what to ask. She blinked rapidly, staring at David drinking from Michael's wrist with shock in her face

Slowly, her gaze shifted to Diego and then to her aunt. Sterling eased his grip on Catherine, exchanging a look with her. Catherine nodded her understanding. She needed to reassure Marcella. "Everything is fine," she said to Marcella with a voice that was pinched a bit. She swiped at her skirt as if needing something to do with her hands. "If you heard my voice, I was overreacting. I'm sorry I disturbed you."

Marcella looked at her aunt for a moment and then let her eyes return to her mate. She'd taken in what Michael was doing with the calmness of a woman who expected the unexpected. And she turned to him and asked for answers, giving him her trust whether she recognized it or not.

"Diego?" She spoke his name in a soft question.

Michael looked at Diego. "Sterling can bandage me. You take care of your woman." Diego nodded.

"He needs to eat."

Diego needed Marcella. He walked towards her. She was tense. Upset. He felt it. She put on a calm exterior for the world but deep inside she was a wreck. At that moment he realized she made a habit of shielding her emotions from others. He wondered what impact holding everything below the surface had on her. She protected everyone as a part of her nature. But when did she allow herself the opportunity to feel and need?

"I'm fine," he said to Sterling. "I need to explain things to Marcella." And to touch her and hold her and make love to her.

"He has to eat, Marcella," Sterling said. "Our metabolism is not like yours. It's critical."

She nodded at Sterling and then looked at Diego. "I'll take care of him."

The minute the adjoining door shut, Sterling looked at Michael. "What the hell was he thinking coming here alone?" His eyes went to Catherine. "Sorry, ma'am."

Michael focused on Sterling's question not his language. "He thought he could explain his reasons for being here if he was alone. To make the Arions think he only traveled to visit family. He hoped to slip out of the country, with Marcella by his side, with little or no attention."

Catherine was listening intently, concerned but calm beyond reason. She felt good about these men. Especially Diego. She'd often hoped for a man who could watch out for her niece. David wasn't that person though she knew he wanted to be. He simply wasn't what Marcella needed. It took a unique person to understand what her niece faced in her life. Someone like Diego.

And though she knew these men were strong and honorable, she needed to know more. "Marcella is in grave danger, isn't she?" she asked, wanting to know what faced them. It was easier than wondering.

"Yes," Sterling said. "But she is in good hands. You can trust us to take care of her."

"And David?" she asked, concerned for the loyal friend who had been willing to die for someone he cared about.

Michael answered though he still held his wrist at David lips. "He's responding well, but he must return quickly to our main lab to complete the process. He is too weak to only undergo a partial conversion."

Sterling answered. "The sooner the better. In fact I wonder if we shouldn't have a few of our men take him on to the main lab."

"No. I don't want to weaken our manpower. Come bandage me," Michael said to Sterling. "Then I want to scout. Just as the Arions can't sense us down here, we can't sense them."

"What do you mean?" Catherine asked. She'd picked up pieces of information about why they had moved hotels, but no one had completely explained. Everything had happened in a whirlwind. "Down here?"

Sterling walked toward Michael. "Once one of our kind has a sense for you, tracking is easy. Unless you're underground."

"So anywhere Marcella goes, they can find her?"

"If it's above ground," Sterling explained. "And not just Marcella. Anyone one of us can be tracked once on the Arion radar. We have an entire underground facility. More than one, actually. Marcella will be safe there." He pulled tape tight around Michael's wrist. "The critical part is getting her there."

"Are they..." Catherine broke off, her fingers twisting together in front of her. She worried for Marcella. And she often felt tortured by her responsibility to her. By the fear of failing her. "Waiting for us?"

Sterling cut the tape. "Yes, but we know they are. Of course, they know we know as well. It's a standoff of sorts. Healing this child is a big risk."

"Marcella will insist you stay for this family," Catherine warned.

"So we've been told," Michael said. "We understand and plan to be ready for anything that comes our way. Right now, we're going to bring one of our men in to stay with you."

Sterling walked to the door and opened it. A big man with sandy brown hair stepped through the door. He looked a lot like Zorro, with long raven hair and dark skin. "This is Marcus. You'll be safe with him. Sterling and I have some preparing to do."

Catherine looked at this new visitor. A scar traveled the left side of his cheek. He was silent. Not that a man like him needed to speak. His presence would never be missed. He looked stern and dangerous.

She didn't want to think about the "what ifs"...like what if all of these men were really the bad guys. She didn't think so, but how could she be sure? Letting out a breath, she walked to David's side. Staring down at one of the few people she called a friend, she asked, "Will he have a hard time traveling?"

"A couple hours from now, he'll be walking around," Michael said.

Catherine's gaze lifted to Michael's, surprise in her face. Then she refocused on David and took his hand. It was cold. "How can that be? He looks so pale."

"Our world is not what you would call normal," Sterling replied.

Catherine squeezed David's fingers. "Then we fit well together. Nothing about my world is normal."

* * * * *

Hours later, Sterling stood between Michael and Marcus at the edge of the woods, careful to stay a distance from the hotel as they scanned for the enemy. Sterling had really hoped to kick a little Arion ass tonight. Apparently, he wasn't going to get that little treat quite yet. They didn't want to draw the Arions to their location.

"Nothing," Michael said. "Not a damn sign of an Arion."

Marcus scanned the area. "They're underground."

Michael looked at him. "They never hide."

"Who says they're hiding?" Marcus said. "I think they're just buying time."

Michael's expression turned thoughtful. "As in waiting for us to bring Marcella out into the open."

"*Exactamente, compadre,*" Marcus said.

Sterling gave him a thoughtful look. "Which means the child has to come to her. I thought we already decided as much."

"*Sí,*" Marcus agreed. "But we don't know how to reach this family."

"David does and he'll be alert soon," Sterling pointed out.

"Even so, we can't just walk into the hotel and go to the child," Michael said. "The Arions will be all over us."

"This family," Marcus said. "How sure are we they are not part of a setup?"

"We aren't sure of anything at this point," Michael inserted.

Sterling shook his head. "In other words we're fucked."

Chapter Nine

Diego pulled the door shut and locked it. Marcella felt the warmth of his arm as it slid around her waist. As with every time he touched her, she marveled at the funny feeling in her stomach. The way he made her feel was unexplainable.

He turned to her, hands on her hips, and looked at her with concern. When he looked at her with such intimacy and so much true concern, it made her heart contract. "Don't you need to rest?"

"Don't you need to eat?"

A slow smile filled his otherwise weary face. "Ah," he said. "That I do, but not near as much as you need to rest. It will be time to meet the child sooner than later."

"I know," she whispered. Time was wearing on her like a heavy cloak. "Why don't you eat while you explain what's going on. Until you do that, I won't rest anyway."

"Okay. You get in bed and I will sit with you while I eat."

She looked at him, wondering if he knew how he tended to order rather than ask. He smiled. This time a true, reach-the-eyes kind of smile. "Please."

She smiled. "That's better. Okay, I'll get in bed if you eat." His brow inched upward. Despite the heaviness of her mood, she found herself laughing. "Please eat."

"Okay," he said. "Since you put it that way."

A few minutes later Marcella watched Diego swallow the last bite of his second sandwich before reaching for a third. "So David will survive?"

"His chances are much higher. I can't promise anything. I can't fully convert him until we get him back to my home lab."

"You're taking him to Nevada?" she asked. "You don't even like him."

He took his plate and set it on the nightstand and then turned to her. "It's never been about like or dislike."

"Then what is it about?" she asked. Everything was so confusing. Diego was like her cornerstone but she hardly knew him.

"You. It's all about you."

"But what if he doesn't want to go?"

"The option is death."

She swallowed, feeling his words like a cold chill down her spine. "Because he needs the rest of this...this transformation?"

"That's part of it," he said, "but like you he is now a target. He will never live in peace. He might as well fight."

Everything she knew was gone. Nothing would ever be the same. She'd lived such an uprooted life as it was. Any form of stability felt important. "What if I don't want to go?"

"Marcella, you know it's not an option. You have to go."

Suddenly all the pressure she was under surfaced. "I don't have to do anything."

He reached for her but she shrugged out of reach and threw the covers back. "You belong with me," he said.

She glared at him. "Says who?"

His eyes narrowed. "You feel our connection."

"Because you make me feel it. Maybe it's some trick of the mind. Stop screwing with my future. David wouldn't even be hurt if it wasn't for you." She felt manipulated and a part of a big game. Like a token someone was moving around. "Did you convert him so I'd have to go to Nevada?"

His eyes flashed with surprise. "I saved him to make you happy. And I didn't make the Arions come. I stopped them from getting to you."

She didn't know what to believe anymore. "Maybe they followed you. Or maybe you're one of them."

"Marcella—"

"Don't," she said. "Don't tell me one more thing I have to know or do. Nothing."

She pushed off the bed before he could reach for her again. Walking to the window, she shoved the curtain aside. And she found a wall. Nothing but a wall painted with a picture of trees and flowers. A fake exterior so those on the lower level could pretend to have the freedoms and beauty of the other visitors.

She felt completely trapped.

Leaning against the window, palms flat on the hot surface, she let her head drop between her shoulders. She forced a deep breath. In. Out. All her life she'd been restricted. She couldn't just live and experience the freedoms of normal people. For the first time since she was very young, she wondered what that might feel like. And she had never, ever questioned what fate had delivered her.

Healing was her world. Her life. Her reason for existing. Somehow she'd made that okay. But now things didn't seem so acceptable. It was as if all the restrictions and forced confinements of her existence had crashed down on top of her. And the very fact that Diego made her want him bothered her. She didn't want to want him. She didn't want to go to Nevada. She didn't want David to be near death in the next room. What she wanted was the peace of a few days before. To get back the feeling of comfort she thought ruled her decisions.

And then he was there. Diego. A stranger who felt like the only form of peace she could find. Yet he also demanded and forced her actions. As much as he called to her, even claimed her as his mate, she wasn't sure if she should trust him. How could she simply give herself to a man who she'd only just met? With the craziness that had erupted around her, it was hard to know what was real and what was false.

Suddenly Diego was there, hands flattening on her stomach. Hips pressing into her backside. She felt the warmth of his breath on her neck and then her ear. Emotion and sensation erupted. The warmth. The sizzle. The complete way he pulled her to him with so little effort. He simply took her by storm.

"I know this is confusing," he murmured. "I wish I could make it easier."

She leaned back into him and her arm went up, around his neck. No matter how she wanted to resist and question his motives, she couldn't. Not when he was touching her. Mate or not, she wanted him in a way no other man had ever evoked.

"Stop acting like you own me," Marcella whispered, but even as she issued the command, she turned to him.

Their lips met and there was no gentleness on either part. She was burning with not only need but also emotion, combustible in its urgency to escape. His tongue slid against hers with a deep thrust, primal and possessive. He was claiming her without words. And damn it, she answered without hesitation, feeling wilder than she had before. She pressed her body into his, reveled at the feel of his hands sliding over her skin. Touching her legs, her hips, her back, and then finally, yes...her breasts. And she wanted them to stay there. Marcella's hands went to his hands, urging him to touch her.

He kneaded the sensitive mounds as she arched into his palms. But it wasn't enough. She reached for her shirt and he helped her tug it over her head. With no bra on, she was ripe for his viewing in a matter of moments. He stood there, staring down at her, his eyes as hot as his touch. Her nipples tightened with painful bliss as his eyes ravished her. And when his fingers touched them, she moaned with the relief and need it created.

"Harder," she demanded, hardly recognizing her voice or the boldness she simply couldn't hold back.

He pinched them, and the jolt of heat shot to her core. The slick wetness of arousal clung to her panties. "Enough?" he asked, his voice hoarse with a sensual hum.

"No," she said, her hands on his wrists as she tried to stabilize herself. "More."

He tugged at her peaks and twisted slightly. "Yes," she whispered. "Yes." But it was so good she thought she would fall. He reacted to her unspoken need and lifted her, his hands cupping her ass. She wrapped her legs around his body, grateful for the steadiness of the bed as he sat her on the edge. He reached for her pants and tugged them down her legs. She wore no panties and was glad. Parting her legs the minute she was free, she invited him into the V of her body. And he was there, hands exploring, and mouth on her neck and shoulder and, God yes, her nipple. Teeth scraping…lips playing.

But as he started to slide farther downward, she had a sudden burst of realization. He was taking her control again and she was letting him. What power might she have over him? Perhaps she needed to find out just what could be done to even the playing field. His fingers slid along the slick folds of her aroused core and she bit back a sound. If she didn't act now, she'd be lost.

Her hands tightened on his head, and he looked up at her. A primal look danced in his eyes, raw and seductive. He was male perfection. She took a deep breath. The thought of taking charge of such a powerful beast—and at the moment that was what he reminded her of—was becoming highly erotic.

"Stand up," she said, firm with her tone.

His eyes narrowed. "I'm not through yet."

Her brow lifted. "Yes, you are. Stand up."

* * * * *

A slow smile just barely lifted his lips before he did as she said. She moved then and pressed her knees into the mattress. "Get undressed."

There was no hesitation. He pulled his t-shirt over his head and gave her a delicious view of his chest. Dark hair sprinkled warm milk chocolate skin. Muscles formed a V tapering to his waist and rippling abs teased with the promise of where they led.

She slid off the bed and to his feet. On her knees, she pressed her lips to his navel and dipped her tongue in it.

Her hands wrapped his hips and she palmed his taut ass. His hands went to her hair, and she heard a soft sound escape his lips. She smiled as her hand slid to his cock and cupped it. Tracking the head with her fingers, she reached for the laces of one of his boots. Eager to touch him but just as eager to get him naked.

She imaged touching his body...holding him in her palm and feeling the throb of his arousal. It pressed her urgently, and she reached for the other boot. Moments later, she looked up at him. "Get rid of them."

He used his feet to kick one off and then the other. She reached for the band of his jeans. "These too."

Soon all barriers were gone. Diego stood before her, his cock long, hard and ready.

Just as she was.

Marcella wrapped her arms around his calves and slowly arched her back so that her tongue touched the tip of his erection. His cock jumped and she smiled. Power. She'd never known it with a man. It was a high. Absolute fire in her veins.

And it made her want to make this last. She slid around him until she was behind his body, still at his feet. And then she stood. Her hands cupped his ass and then slid around his hips as she pressed her breasts into his back. Her teeth scraped the skin. But he was impatient, tugging her around his body and pulling her against his chest. His mouth closed down on hers, ravishing her with a deep plunge of his tongue.

Her hand went to his cock and closed around it. He moaned against her lips and she began pumping him. "Feel good?" she asked in a whispered voice.

"You know it does."

She sucked his bottom lip between her teeth as her fingers found the soft tip of his erection and spread the wetness now present. Her nipples tightened in reaction. Knowing he was this turned on because of her was burning her up. She reached for his hands and pressed them against her breasts, shutting her eyes with the pure bliss of being in his palms.

But she only allowed herself a few seconds to feel. Otherwise she might get lost. There was still too much to do. Too much to feel. Over the edge now would be too soon. She sank back to her knees and again grabbed his calves and touched her tongue to him. Then immediately, before he had time to know what hit him, she circled his head with a flat rough swoosh of her tongue. She looked up at him as she trailed her tongue around and up and down as if he were an ice cream cone. He looked at her, eyes potent with arousal. It turned him on to see his cock in her mouth.

To her amazement, she could feel the wetness between her legs, sizzling with her own burn. She liked this too. Her palms inched up his legs to the back of his powerful thighs. And then his perfect, tight ass. Damn, she liked the man's backside. She caressed it, enjoyed the way he flexed in response. Then she moved her hand and circled his cock with her fingers. He let out a heavy breath as if he'd been holding it, waiting for this moment. Instantly, his hands were on her head. Marcella liked that too. It told her he felt urgent.

She squeezed the base and sucked him deeper into her mouth. A little. Another inch. Slow. Downward she went. Taking him fully until her wet lips connected with her index finger.

His hands went to her hair. She slowly slid back down his length and he arched into her. He pushed his big cock back into her mouth, as if he was afraid she wouldn't do it herself. Marcella sucked harder, loving the power she had to make him feel urgent. To make him fear she wouldn't give him what he wanted. Taking him again as he thrust. Once. Twice. Over and over he moved in and out.

Until he pressed into her mouth with a heavy push of his hips and tossed his head back, a roar of release slipping from his lips.

* * * * *

Diego knew Marcella had just tried to fight the power he had over her with...well, power.

And he liked it. If she wanted to share control on some things, he had no problem with it. Unless it impacted her safety, it was fine by him. On the other hand, he believed in give and get. She had just pleasured him and he damn sure wanted a satisfied mate.

Marcella pushed to her feet and he didn't give her a chance to escape. He slid his arms under her legs and picked her up. "What are you doing?" she asked, startled.

He smiled at her. "Taking you to bed with me where you belong." He shoved back the blankets and settled her on the mattress. She scrambled to a sitting position.

He stared at her, his brow lifting. "Running? Now why would that be?"

"We need to talk, Diego."

He looked at her breasts, high and full, nipples peaked, and felt the hunger of his beast begin to roar again. He'd never get enough of her. "Later. Let's finish what we started first." He started towards her.

She pointed. "Stay right there. I want to talk."

Forcing a deep breath, he tried to pull his body back into control. This was clearly important to her. But his cock was already full and pumping with life. He watched her eyes drop.

"I can't help what you do to me," he said. "But if talking is important we will talk."

He sat on the bed and she scooted farther away. "Marcella, I will never force you to do what you don't want. You have no need to run from me."

Her eyes flashed. "I'm not running."

"Yes, you are."

"No…" She pursed her lips and reached for the sheet, tugging it over her body. "I need to rest."

"I thought you wanted to talk."

"Why are you doing this to me?" she bit out through clenched teeth.

Suddenly, Diego felt like a complete ass. He'd mated with Marcella because he knew it was an extra line of defense. He would be stronger and she would be more powerful. But forcing the emotional components of their bond was something he couldn't justify. Everything that had just happened between them had been about Marcella trying to regain control over her life.

Something she perceived he had taken.

"Marcella, honey, I'm not trying to do anything to you. And I don't want to pressure you." He reached for his pants.

"Are…are you leaving?"

Diego gave her a reassuring look. "No. I'm going to sit on that chair in the corner and let you rest." He used his chin to motion towards the bed. "Rest. I'll be here if you need me."

She stared at him a long moment and then slid down under the blankets. He walked to the wall and flipped the light off. Then he went to the corner chair and sat down. The physical part of their relationship was hard to fight for either of them. But emotional part was another story. He owed her time to adjust and allow herself to understand what she felt.

And he was going to give it to her. His head fell back against the back of his seat and he let his eyes close. Her smell was soft and feminine and it called to him. He so wanted to hold her and tell her he loved her. But he knew he had to give her this space. As tempting as it was, he didn't even allow himself to reach for her mind. Yet he felt the warmth of her presence and knew she touched his. And he let her. This was his mate. She needed to see he was true in his feelings.

"Diego?"

"Yes?"

"You need to rest too."

"I'm fine. I am."

Silence.

"Come lay with me," she whispered.

He sat up and found her doing the same. "I'm fine here."

"I want you to."

Diego wasn't sure how to respond.

"Come lay with me."

He pushed to his feet and walked towards her. She lifted the blanket and he stopped beside the bed. Leaving his clothes on seemed the best way to offer her the security of control. He slid down beside her, on his back, and smiled as she snuggled to his side.

His hand stroked her hair, and the warmth of their connection washed over him. "Goodnight, Marcella."

Chapter Ten

ॐ

Diego stared at the ceiling for a long while. He'd slept an hour, which was plenty. His body allowed him to go days with very little sleep. He knew he needed to go check on David. His mind was also heavy with concerns. Like how to get the child and Marcella together with the least amount of danger. Hopefully, David would be awake now so they could get the rundown on how to contact the family.

He gently eased Marcella off his shoulder. She reached for him. "What? Where are you going?"

He touched her hair, offering a reassuring touch. "I'll be back. I'm just going to make sure everything is as it should be."

She looked like she would argue and then she eased back onto the pillow. He stood above her, staring down at her a long moment. At the woman who held his heart and his body. And silently he vowed to win her love. To give her time and space and never force an emotional attachment. They were mates. With the passing of days, she would accept what they felt for one another was natural. A gift most would never experience. What they shared was unique. He'd seen how the Knights' leader, Mason, had changed with his mate by his side. He'd embraced his powers and grown into his potential.

And with Marcella by his side, he would fight for the future with renewed vigor.

He walked to the adjoining doors and quietly pulled the door open, careful not to wake anyone. But no one was asleep. Not even David. Diego shut the door behind him and stepped into the room. The tension in the air was thick.

"What's wrong?" he asked of them all.

"Not one Arion to be detected," Sterling answered, running a hand through his long blond hair. "They must be underground."

"Waiting on us," Diego said, feeling the certainty of his words.

"Yes," Michael said. "Waiting. I know she wants to heal this child, but we are risking a lot to make this happen."

Diego knew he was right, but if he didn't make this happen for Marcella, he'd never win her heart. And the Knights might not win her help. "We'll have to bring the child to us. We have to do this." He looked at David. "What are the specifics of the meeting?"

David pushed to a sitting position. "We're to go to the family's room."

"Which isn't an option," Sterling said with a tight voice.

"Right," Michael said. "Unless..." His eyes went to Catherine where she stood by David's bed.

Her eyes went wide. "Me?" She swallowed and then nodded. "I can do it. You mean they can't track me?"

"You're the only one in question," Michael explained. "We know they can find all the Knights. We sense our kind automatically. But you are both human and perhaps unknown at this point. We need a good plan, but you might be the only one who has a chance of not being noticed. I don't think they have your presence memorized yet."

Diego walked to a chair and sat down. "The Arions came to the hotel the day I arrived. They might have been following Marcella. Catherine was with her. I think it's too risky."

"It's our only chance of going unnoticed," Michael said in a flat tone. "The girl has to come to us and we can't risk the phone lines. That means Catherine has to deliver a message."

"We really shouldn't be doing this at all," Sterling interjected.

David's head turned sharply as he fixed Sterling in a hard stare. "Marcella will never agree to leave without helping that child."

Sterling wasn't one to back down. Diego knew what was coming even before Sterling issued his challenge. "And if she dies trying, what does that do for any of us?"

Catherine interjected. "I'll do it." Her eyes skirted around the room. "Whatever it is you need me to do, I'll do it."

Diego let his elbows rest on his knees. What the hell was he supposed to do? He felt damned if he did and damned if he didn't. Michael fixed him in a steady stare. "Can I talk to you in the hall?"

Diego nodded and pushed to his feet. He walked to the door with both Michael and Sterling following. He trusted them both completely. And so did Mason, their leader. They were his right and left arms. Michael tended to take charge. It was simply his nature. For Diego, it was about medicine, science and healing. He fought when necessary. A warrior by nature he wasn't. This alone made him get along well with Michael. Neither stepped on each other's toes. But at times they had different agendas. He feared this was one of those times.

Once they were in the hall, door closed to the others, Michael spoke. "We have a problem."

Diego's jaw firmed. "I know."

"No," Michael said. "Another one."

Diego's brow inched upward.

"Holly is sick," Sterling offered. "Throwing up for twelve hours straight. Mason says she's not doing well."

Diego's gut tightened. There was no way to talk to Mason again for hours. They had set times they called. A timing device scrambled the phone line and kept it from being traced. It sent waves in the air that blocked the Arion detectors. A brilliant discovery by one of their tech men. But the Arions adapted anything that occurred on a constant level. It only worked at random interval settings and for two-minute windows.

Diego took a deep breath. He'd recently added a junior physician to his team but this was beyond what normal medical experience prepared for. Giving birth to a child of another species was no small miracle.

"Jason's a good doctor," Diego said, but he wasn't sure if he was reassuring Michael and Sterling or himself.

Several moments of silence passed.

"Well, the bottom line is we have a lot of reason to get the hell out of here," Sterling said.

"Right," Diego agreed. He pressed two fingers to the bridge of his nose and thought a moment. "If we don't make this happen, Marcella isn't going to come with us willingly. And she might be exactly what Holly needs.

Besides, she has new powers since mating with me. She can help us I think. Meditation of some sort is her control point. We can learn from her."

"You're sure she can heal?" Sterling asked. "I'm concerned about Holly and the impact losing her would have on Mason."

"Positive." Diego didn't have to say more. They all knew she was his mate. It was something that males sensed. They knew their mate and they knew when someone belonged to another.

Sterling sighed. "I say we send Catherine."

With heaviness in his heart, Diego had to agree. "Right. It's our only option."

"Agreed," Michael said. "The question is where do we meet up with the child?"

Sterling added, "And when."

Not quick enough, Diego thought. He had a bad feeling about all of this. The sooner he had Marcella back at their main lab, the better. And if anything happened to Catherine, he worried about how Marcella would respond.

He could only hope and pray nothing went wrong. Because losing Marcella would not only kill him, it could destroy Mason. Without him, the Knights would be weak and the Arions strong.

* * * * *

Diego stood with his entire team, including Marcella and her aunt, in the hotel parking garage. It was just before sunrise, and they were ready to set a plan into action. Nerves were on edge. Tension was high. Expressions sullen.

A mud-stained van sat beside them. Sterling and Michael had acquired it from a border town equipped with an abundance of toys. The kind made for games of war. The doors stood open, exposing a gutted interior and walls lined with weapons.

Catherine had just been wired with a bug. Diego found her to be a woman of strength. She showed no fear for the task ahead of her. Only courage and readiness. Well hidden beneath her blouse, the device would allow them to know what was happening to and around her as she experienced it. The expensive audio equipment tucked neatly in the front dash of the van would keep her in range.

"Just remember," Diego said, placing a calming hand on Catherine's shoulder. "Everything you say or hear we will too. We are always only moments away from helping."

"That's not true," Marcella argued, distress etched her tone. "You said you can't get close or they will sense your presence."

Diego looked at her, ensuring she saw the truth in his eyes. "We have exceptional speed. I wouldn't promise what we can't deliver."

Sterling focused on David. "Shoot them in the head or they don't die." He handed David a standard Glock 17 9mm semiautomatic pistol. "Anyplace else just pisses them off. And they travel with the wind. You blink and they will be on your ass."

David took the weapon and then stuck it in a vest he'd strapped to his body. "Meaning what exactly? How fast are they? What am I dealing with?"

"With the wind was quite literal. We, like the Arions, can become the wind but only for short distances."

Marcella turned to Diego and spoke to him with their mental connection. *Can you –*

He was pleased to have her speak to him so privately. It was acceptance of their bond whether she recognized it or not. *Yes.*

Her brows dipped. *Can I?*

Not yet.

Unless he did a blood exchange with her she would remain half human. He wanted that to be her choice. He'd decided the night before, he'd been small minded about their mating. A partial bonding was for her safety. Complete joining would be her option. It was a hard decision because she would be safer with full GTECH enhancements. But would she be happier?

Marcella looked as if she might question him further, but David was talking again, pulling her attention. "I'm supposed to shoot someone in the head that has claws," he held up a finger, "I know this from firsthand knowledge, I remind you. And now I find they also travel with the wind. Right?" His lips thinned. "Exactly how the hell am I supposed to get to their head before they're on me?"

Michael pulled a gun from his jacket. It was one of many strapped to his body in various places. "This shoots tranquilizers." David took it. "The trick is to stun them so they can't use their powers and then shoot them in the head."

Catherine was staring at Michael's wrist. "Your bandage is gone. And your arm…"

"Is healed," Michael answered.

Diego walked to the van and grabbed a belt and turned to Catherine. They didn't have time to explain their differences. Right now they needed to talk about things that would save lives. "Strap this to your waist. Have you ever fired a gun?"

"She's sixty, Diego. This is crazy. She can't do this."

"I know how to shoot," Catherine said and then fixed Marcella in a look. "I'm fine, *hija*. Trust me."

"What?" Marcella asked, surprised. "You know how to shoot?"

"Yes," Catherine said. "And I should have made sure you did. I was foolish to think I could shelter you from the world. It didn't work for your mother, and it has failed you as well."

"I don't want to learn how to shoot. No." She hugged herself. "I heal people. I don't kill them."

"These aren't people," Michael said, pulling another gun from his jacket. "They're Arions. Cold-blooded killers." He held the gun out to her. "Kill or be killed. You choose."

She stared at his hand. Diego resisted pressing her. He was thankful Michael had posed this issue rather than him. He felt he had been the bad guy in her eyes far too much.

"Take it," Catherine said. "Do not be a fool, child."

Marcella looked at her aunt for several long moments and then reached for the gun. "Tell me what to do."

Diego grabbed a vest from the van and held it up behind her. Marcella allowed him to slip it around her. He turned her to face him and he clipped the front into place. His hand slid to the metal in hers. "I'll show you after everyone is in position. We'll have some down time." He then slid the weapon into her vest. And then he reached for his tranquilizer gun and stuck it in the opposite side of the jacket. "Left you have bullets. Right is to stun. For now get used to thinking about what is what. Right first. Left second."

"I'm not a killer," she whispered.

"Neither am I. But I'm a survivor and so are you."

*****

The parking garage was pitch-black. You'd never know the sun had just shown itself beyond the concrete walls. Marcella sat on the floor of the broken-down van, knuckles balled by her sides. Diego sat directly across from her. He, like her, wore jeans and tennis shoes. He'd insisted she dress in clothes that would be easy to move around in. She knew he was anticipating trouble. His uneasiness hummed like a live charge.

"I can't believe we're making this child travel," she said, wishing this was over.

"It's the only way," Diego said in a low voice.

"I should have gone to her."

"The Arions would have grabbed you before you got to her."

Sterling guarded the outside along with two newly arrived Knights. David was in the driver's seat of the van ready to make a fast escape. Michael and Marcus had gone with her aunt along with several other Knights she'd met only a few minutes ago. "Are you sure we can trust all of these people?"

"Michael knows them. That's enough for me."

Marcella nodded. Words wouldn't come. She'd learned to shoot a gun the best she could in a short lesson. Wanting to use it was the hard part. "It's been a long time since my aunt went inside the hotel. Shouldn't we know something by now?"

Before Diego could answer, a thundering noise sounded on the side of the van. Marcella jumped, heart beating at double time. The door flew open. Sterling was the first thing she saw. And in his arms was the child. Long black hair hung around her pale face. Marcella's chest tightened as the girl's pain wrapped around her heart.

She pushed to her knees and waved him forward. "Bring her to me."

Sterling laid her on the floor of the van and Marcella moved to her side. Her finger brushed wispy strands of hair from her eyes. "It's okay, little one." She looked up at Sterling. "Where are the parents?"

"I made them wait in their car."

She nodded. "Good. Their fear will distract me."

He gave her a quick bob of his chin and shoved the doors shut. Marcella placed her hand on the child's forehead and her breath caught. The poison was potent. She felt it like acid in her veins. Fear clenched at her heart. As tired and distracted as she was, she wasn't sure she could do this.

But then Diego was there in her mind. *I'm with you. Tell me what to do.*

At first she resisted the intrusion. Even wanted to scream at him for daring such an invasion. But a warm feeling of control came over her, making her limbs tingle.

Like a calming drug. A breath, then two and she knew Diego had just made her stronger.

She relaxed and went to work reaching inside the child's body with her mind.

* * * * *

"Now?"

Damion looked at the man to his left. "Not yet. Let her finish with the child."

Damion smiled from the far corner of the parking garage. Things were going just as he planned. The woman would be weak after she healed the child. He'd done his homework. Nothing this big should be approached unprepared.

Soon he would take his prize to his king.

Chapter Eleven

❧

Diego had never experienced anything like this before in his life. Marcella had placed her hand on the child's head and he had felt what she did. When she had accepted his assistance the feeling had doubled. He had nearly doubled over in pain, so raw was the ache in the child's body. And somehow, someway, Marcella had absorbed it into her body and then poured the disease into the air around them. Like smoke being burned off a flame.

When she had finally lifted her hand, he had found himself breathing heavily. It had taken him a moment to pull himself back to the present. "Call for the parents," Marcella whispered, easing herself against the wall of the van. Exhaustion etched her face. "She needs to sleep but she'll make it."

He nodded, but he too felt the heaviness of what had just occurred though not to the extreme Marcella did. A few minutes later, Sterling shut the doors to the van as another Knight carried the child to her parents. Diego went to Marcella and pulled her close. They relaxed into each other.

"Thank you," Marcella whispered. "I couldn't have done it without you."

But then Sterling yelled. Diego stiffened, but Marcella was too weak to respond. The door to the van jerked open but Diego was prepared. He shoved Marcella behind him and rose to his knees. Both guns drawn, he aimed at his target.

He wasn't going down without a fight.

"Don't shoot! *No disparden!*"

A gray-haired older man stood before him, thin and weary looking. His hands trembled as he held them palms up in front of his body. Sterling appeared behind him. "It's okay. It's the father. I told him to stop. He wanted to thank Marcella."

The man spoke in a fast string of Spanish and then tears fell down his cheeks. "*Muchas gracias, señorita. Muchas gracias.*"

Diego let out a breath and let his weapons drop. David cursed behind him, clearly as rattled as he was. His gaze moved to Marcella and to his complete surprise, he realized she held a weapon. As tired as she was, she had managed to draw one of her guns. She was still sitting but twisted to face the front.

She let the gun fall to her side. "I so hate what I'm becoming." Her eyes locked with Diego's. "I could have killed him."

Diego's gut twisted because her words held accusation. As if she blamed him. "Marcella—"

The father began speaking again, rambling words of thanks. Marcella turned slowly to face him and spoke to him in Spanish. Her words were soft as she assured him his daughter would be fine and told him to take her home.

Diego stayed on alert, feeling unsettled. Perhaps it was Marcella's anger towards him. He wasn't sure. He simply felt uncomfortable. But even as the father turned away and Sterling disappeared with him, Diego couldn't make himself pull back from alert position.

Something wasn't right. "David, start the van."

"What? I thought we were waiting on the others?"

Every sense he owned was on alert. The Arions were underground. They had to be. He felt something was wrong but he couldn't get a read. "Start the damn van."

Diego moved to shut the van doors and spoke to Marcella. "Right gun first. Left second."

But it was too late. Two Arions stepped in front of the van door, both holding machine guns. One he knew all too well. "Hello, Diego."

Diego stared at their visitor. "Hello, Damion."

And then the guns went off and everything went black.

* * * * *

"No!"

Marcella's eyes opened and her heart hammered against her chest. And all she saw was darkness. Cold, wet darkness. She'd been dreaming. No. That was no dream. It had been a nightmare. She'd killed the father. The man who only wanted to save his child. Like a cold-blooded murderer she had shot him dead.

She forced a long, bitter breath and the disorientation began to ease. It had been a dream. A damp kind of chill slid along her arms. It brought with it the ache of her limbs pressed hard behind her back. She blinked several times and tried to move her hands, but rope held them bound behind her back.

Realization came with a sudden rush. The van. The Arions. The child's father. Had he gotten away safely? Oh…the child. What if she had been hurt? Marcella reached for memories. She'd almost shot the father. But she hadn't. No. No. No. She remembered. It was only in her nightmare that she had shot him. She sucked in a breath. But it had still been a horrible thing, what she had done. To hold a weapon on a man and almost take his life. An innocent man who meant no harm. She was a healer not a murderer.

But then those monsters had appeared and she had forgotten the fear of pulling the trigger. She had wanted to kill. To take their lives. Yet she'd been so weak. And they had been so fast. Within a blink of an eye bullets were flying in the air and she had felt the prick of metal…known they were all dying.

But they hadn't been bullets. They had been shot with tranquilizer darts. Put to sleep and then captured.

And now she was tied to a chair. Where they had been taken she didn't know. Her eyes were adjusting. She blinked and her eyes skirted around the room. Carved walls and jagged rocks surrounded her. It looked like some sort of cave or tunnel. David was across from her tied up and unconscious. As was her aunt and Sterling. Their heads hung forward heavy with sleep or drugs. But they were alive and it offered relief.

Where were the others? Had they somehow avoided capture? Diego. Oh God, Diego. Where was he? She felt a rush of panic and forced a deep breath. Focus. "Focus," she murmured.

Another deep breath later, she reached for his mind. And she found blankness. No! Diego! Nonononono… Her stomach twisted in a knot. Please don't let him be dead. She squeezed her eyes shut and tried again. It was hard to focus. She wasn't sure how much time had gone by but it had to have been a while because she no longer felt the effects of healing the child. The leaden feeling in her mind was drug induced, she was certain. It made it hard to function, but she needed to find Diego. Slowly, she felt the low hum of his presence. It slowed her heartbeat and made her breathe easier. He was alive but knocked out like the others. Somehow, she had to wake him up. She began calling his name in her mind.

* * * * *

Diego's eyes opened and his head snapped upward. "Marcella."

"Ah yes, Marcella. Your mate. Your life. Your very breath. How sweet."

The voice of Damion brought everything back to Diego. He'd been at the Area 51 camp for hours now. They'd been torturing him for information. For the Knight home location, new discoveries and battle plans. His chest was sliced open. He didn't have to look down to remember. The dull throb of the wound brought the memory back to him as did the stickiness clinging to his skin.

"Fuck you, Damion."

Diego said the words but focused on his immediate concern. Sterling. His eyes went to him and he found his head tilted backwards. Blood trickled down his neck. So newly converted, healing wasn't as easy for him, and he needed extra nutrients. He reached for his mind, feeling the pain and knowing he had to shield him from it. But if he did, would he have the energy to fight?

"Perhaps," Damion said, drawing his attention, "Marcella is the way to make you talk. If we torture her I believe you might just come to your senses."

Anger, pain and even fear sliced through his heart. "If you touch her, I'll kill you."

Damion laughed and walked towards him. "You would like that, wouldn't you?" he taunted. His voice was as evil as was the source. Diego had never liked him. He knew Damion from his days stuck with the Arions. Before he managed to join the Knights in the battle against them.

"I will do it. Mark my word," Diego promised.

Diego stared at Damion. With short brown hair and a short, flat nose, he resembled a pit bull. Even his body was corded and thick like an animal's. A product of steroids and enhancement combined. He'd been massive even before the enhancements. So much so that he had moved awkwardly. But with the injections and transition to Arion he'd gained speed.

Even so, Diego knew he was a big chicken shit. Though he was powerful, he rarely battled. He stood back and watched others do his dirty work. But not this time. Diego was damn well going to get free and when he did…

"You're weak," Damion said, as if responding to the silent anger in Diego's mind. "No food. No source of vitamin C. I doubt very seriously you will be doing much of anything but crying."

He was tied to a chair, arms behind his back. Beside him was Sterling who had been just as tight-lipped. Neither of them had eaten nor had they consumed enough vitamin C. Their bodies were depleted and they had both been beaten. Yet he knew he had to find the power to fight.

Damion now stood in front of him. A knife extended from his wrist. And with a quick swipe of his wrist he sliced Diego's jaw. He felt the pain of the moment.

"And you're bleeding." He smiled. "Not good for a weak body. But I think you leave me no choice. We will torture you. If it doesn't work, we will move on to your mate."

Damion's eyes slid to Sterling and he moved towards him. He stopped in front of Sterling and looked down at him. "But first—"

His words were cut off as Sterling raised his head and spit in his face. "Bastard. Untie me and fight me like a man."

Damion hissed and his teeth extended. Fangs were nice little weapons only more advanced Arions possessed. But it was with his knifed hand that he lashed out, slicing Sterling as he had Diego, across the face. Sterling's head jerked with the impact. Blood was matted in his long blond hair. His skin was pale. Dark circles beneath his eyes showed heavy bruising.

"You're not worth wasting my breath on," Damion spat at Sterling, looking ready to lash out again. "You can't take one blow from me."

Sterling laughed, but it held a hoarse feel of pain. Diego knew he had to stop this now. Sterling was called the Renegade for a reason. He almost welcomed death. It was like he had a point in life and it was death.

Damion raised his hand to hit him again and then stopped, hand midair. A slow smile slid onto his face.

Two other Arions stepped forward as if they were answering some call. Diego didn't know them but he did know their fists. Damion held up a staying hand. "Wait. I just had a brilliant idea." He fixed Diego in a hard stare. "Oh yes. This is perfect. Here is what I am going to do. Either tell me what I want to know or…"

Chapter Twelve

ဆ

"David!" Marcella had called his name and her aunt's over and over. Both had stirred but neither actually responded. Her nerves were on edge. She needed help here. Even Diego wouldn't answer her calls. But Marcella felt him in a stronger way now. She clung to that as hope.

She searched the room, looking for anything she could use to free her hands, but there was nothing. She needed David to wake up. There was a bottle on the ground. An empty orange juice container. She frowned. Why did everyone drink juice? Shoving the thought aside, she focused. The bottle moved and then lifted before flying at David. It smashed into his shoulder and fell to the ground.

His head moved. She felt her heart jump. "David! David!"

He slowly raised his head but his eyes didn't move. She called to him again. And then with a flutter his lashes lifted. At that moment she felt so much better. "Where…are we?"

But before she could answer, the steel door that enclosed them rattled. And then Diego was being carried into the room attached to a chair. They dumped him sideways onto the ground. He groaned at the same moment Marcella gasped. She felt his pain like none other she'd ever experienced. It might have been her own it was so alive with force. Her chest ached. Her head. Her face.

"Diego," she whispered.

I'm sorry, Marcella.

Even as she reached for Diego's mind, trying to ease his pain, Sterling was flung on his side, also tied to a chair. She heard David curse and then a man stood in the doorway. A huge, ugly man with a flat nose.

"You can thank your mate for this," he said with a snide bite to his voice. A satisfied smile slid onto his lips.

Marcella had a twisting feeling in her gut.

Marcella. Diego whispered in her mind but she didn't look at him. She was afraid to look away from the evil before her. *Marcella. I had no choice.*

And then suddenly two of the monsters were grabbing her aunt. She moaned and her lashes fluttered. "What are you doing?" Marcella yelled. "Put her down. Where are you taking her? No!" She kept calling out to them. And Diego kept whispering in her head.

"Thank Diego. I gave him a choice. Really two choices. Tell me what I wanted to know or I would kill someone. I even let him choose who." He laughed. "And he chose your aunt."

Her chest tightened and she couldn't find her breath or even her voice. But the door started to shut and her aunt was leaving her…forever… "Nooo!"

* * * * *

If he weren't on the ground, lying on his damn side, life at this very fucking moment would feel a hell of a lot better. Or not. Shit. Marcella was screaming at the door for her aunt. And he knew the instant her attention was on him even before her words lashed out at him. He couldn't see her face, only David's.

"I hate you!" she screamed. "I can't believe you did this. How could you let them take her! How could you choose her? Let them take me! Wh—"

"Marcella." The harsh order came from David. "Calm down and let Diego speak. And Sterling is about to bleed to death on us."

Diego could hear her breathing hard. And he could feel her shock at David's words. Silence filled the cave. "Let's give the man a chance to explain."

"You of all people are telling me to give him a chance," Marcella bit out. Her tone was low and controlled now but no less intense.

"He saved my life," David said softly. "He earned a chance to explain himself. At least from me he did."

"This is what they want, Marcella," Diego said. "I either had to join the Arions with you by my side or they would ensure you hated me enough to join them alone."

"What does that mean for my aunt?" she whispered. Then louder. "What did you let them do to her?"

It hurt to even say the words. The choice had been hell. "I had to choose which person in this room died first."

"And you chose my aunt? The little old lady? What kind of man are you?"

Sterling's voice came with the muffled sound of a swollen lip. "The kind that got the shit beat out of him because he refused to answer. But then they promised to rape you in front of him. He had no choice."

Marcella started to respond. "So—"

"Marcella," Diego said in a low voice. "I beg of you. Put aside your emotions and focus. I am weak and so is

Sterling. If you and I do not bind our powers we will all die here in this cave."

"Not true," Sterling said. "Marcella will live. They have plans for her."

"What plans?" Marcella said. "What does that mean?"

"You know they want you," Diego said. "Right now we all need you." He paused. "I need you."

* * * * *

Marcella wasn't sure what to do. Or really what she felt. All she knew was she wanted her aunt to live. Diego's words played in her mind. *I need you.* Well, she needed her aunt. Yet a tiny voice in her mind called her to reason. She could find her aunt and help her. First, she had to get untied and out of this place.

"Fine," Marcella said. "What do I need to do?"

Silence. She didn't like it. Marcella knew he wasn't well. As much as she wanted to hate him right now, she knew she felt something quite the opposite. Needing to know he was okay, she cried out to him, but instinct made her do it with her mind. *Diego!*

Yes, mi hermosa, I am here.

Even in her head, he seemed tired. Exhausted. She wondered if he spoke in her head because he lacked the ability to find his voice. Marcella forced away the fear for her aunt. There wasn't time to meditate. She had to find her power and her focus right here. Right now.

And as if he heard her question, Diego responded. *This is what you need to do. Reach for my mind with yours. We must combine our powers. I am far too weak to do this alone.*

What do you mean weak? She tried to focus on his body. On his injuries. *How badly are you hurt?*

Let's focus on what's important —

"We need a plan, damn it!" It was Sterling sounding rather irritated. "I don't especially like the view here with my face smashed to the ground!"

"We *are* talking," Marcella said. "Just wait a minute. Give us time."

Sterling mumbled something hard to understand and ended with, "Hurry up. I might not be experienced at this mind reading shit but I can bet we don't have a whole hell of a lot of time."

Focus here, Marcella. On me. We need to combine powers. I have no idea what we can do together. You had powers as did I before we connected but we are not fully bound.

What?

I'll explain later but basically you won't have all of my powers.

"Can't you two travel with the wind?" David asked.

"You detect a breeze, dipshit?" Sterling asked, clearly getting more on edge by the minute. "And you think we'd just leave you two here?"

Diego spoke to Marcella before she could reply to them. *Ignore them. We need to get them untied. Use your mind. Imagine what you want to happen. Visualize it in your mind.*

Her brows dipped. *Like the ropes melting away?*

Right. Let's try. Reach for my mind and I will yours.

I've never done anything like this. Marcella felt her heart kick up a beat. What if she failed? No. What if they failed?

Focus. Don't think about 'what ifs'.

And like a warm blanket Diego was there in her mind, calming her. She wanted to hate him, but with the intimate touch of their connection she felt safe. Capable. Able to do this. She closed her eyes and focused…

To her shock and amazement her ropes loosened and then freedom. Her arms warmed with the blood flow. Lifting her hands, she stared at them and then around the room. David was free.

Sterling moved his hands to the floor in front of him. "About damn time." He pushed to a sitting position, blood matted to his cheek. "What other tricks can you two do?"

Marcella looked at Diego who now was sitting. Their eyes locked. In that moment, she wanted to tell him she loved him. But she didn't. He sent her aunt to death or some worse fate like torture. She should hate him for it. Instead she hated herself.

What kind of woman wanted a man who taught her to kill and cared so little for her only living family?

* * * * *

After the ropes had disappeared, Diego was confident in what he and Marcella could do together. If only she and David were converted fully. If they could travel with the wind, they could be to the Knight lab in no time.

But they couldn't, which meant options were limited.

Diego went to Marcella and settled his hands on her arms. Her fingers went to his cheek. "It's deep. You need stitches."

"I'm fine," he said, but he knew he wasn't. His hand went to hers, drawing it away from his face. He was weak. Each push with his mind was making him more so. But touching Marcella gave him a sense of power. As if together they were stronger. And maybe they were. "Here is our real test," he told her. "When we open that door, we have to make the camera think we didn't. I think we should divide and conquer. Merge our minds and then think of different tasks. I'll open the door. You make the camera think it doesn't open."

"How do you know this place?" she asked. "Where are we?"

"I'll explain later, but we aren't in Mexico anymore. We're in Nevada, and for the first time in a long time, I'm thankful I have intimate knowledge of what obstacles these walls represent. If we get past this camera there will be two more."

Her eyes went wide. "But how will we know if I'm successful?"

"We won't." It was the simple truth and he saw no reason to hide it. "We just have to hope."

He turned to the door, taking her hand in his. David and Sterling stood side by side. Both looked like shit, but Sterling was by far in the worst shape. He needed food, vitamin C and sleep. All the more reason they had to make this work.

Diego looked at Marcella, a question in his eyes. She nodded and they turned to the door. They had to make this happen.

* * * * *

The door had opened and the Arions had never known a thing. Diego knew the compound like the back of his hand. Getting them out of the facility had been the hard part. But he knew places others wouldn't. Ways to get to the outskirts of the camp unseen.

Now they were at the point of no return, to the edge of the woods that would lead them to safety. Diego stopped, knowing it was time to part with Marcella. He'd kept Marcella close as they had traveled, her hand in his. Three times she had tried to turn back. Each time she'd spoke in his mind, begging him to save her aunt.

He looked at Sterling. "I am trusting you with her life."

Sterling shook his head. "You can't go back on your own."

"They won't even know I was there."

"I'm going with you," Marcella said. "We are stronger together. Our power. You need our power."

Diego turned to her. "No. You go with Sterling and David. I'll bring Catherine back to you." He hesitated. This was what his mate wanted. He felt her anguish and pain. "Or I'll die trying."

"I'll go with you," David said.

Diego looked at the man he had considered an enemy. Now he regretted the harshness of his shortsighted behavior. He patted David on the shoulder. "No, my new friend. You must go and heal. Your body is weak." He paused. "And if I do not return, keep her safe."

Marcella grabbed his arm. "Don't go alone. You can't go alone. No. Please."

"I have to. Sterling and David are in no shape to come with me. Besides, Sterling is the only one who knows how to get you to safety." Diego looked at him but spoke to Marcella. "Get food down him and fast."

"I'm the one you need." She grabbed the front of his shirt and stepped close. "We work well together and I'm fine."

"I thought you hated me."

"I...I need to go with you."

"You need to go care for Holly. If we lose Mason's mate, this battle will not fare well. We need him and he needs her." Diego grabbed her and pulled her close. "Heal Holly for me. That is all I ask. I will get Catherine."

And before she could protest he kissed her. Long and hard, he thrust his tongue against hers, absorbing all she was...afraid it would be the last taste he ever had.

The wind kicked up around them, tossing dirt around before he could force himself to lift his lips from hers. He'd already begun to fade into the wind. And when the moment came, he touched her cheek and whispered her name.

Praying she would make it to safety.

Chapter Thirteen

ೲ

Marcella couldn't believe how amazing being at a cave in the middle of nowhere felt. But when Sterling announced they had arrived at their destination, she had been ready to shout for joy. Only she had no energy. She watched as he moved a tree limb and did something to the wall. To her amazement a door slid open right smack in the middle of the side of the cave.

Sterling motioned with his chin. "Home sweet home." The words came out weakly. Almost a whisper.

She'd gotten a feel for Sterling's personality. He was not well, yet he tried to make light of the moment. It was his way. Hers was to remain calm. Memories of her panic when the Arions took Catherine flashed in her mind. Okay, so she used to be calm. She didn't know what she was now other than tired and worried.

Inside the cave, she felt the closing of the cave entrance like a tight glove. Darkness surrounded her and seemed to suffocate. A flutter of nerves lifted in her stomach. But then a light flashed and a bit in the distance she saw Sterling standing in the warm glow. Another wall slid open.

And Marcella knew she was about to enter a new world. One where everything known to her was lost. The question was, would Diego be a part of that loss?

* * * * *

Mason stood in the doorway of the lab looking at Holly. She was doubled over with stomach pains yet she still worked. She was the most hardheaded woman he'd ever known.

"Please rest, Holly." His voice held a plea.

She carried his child, though she barely looked pregnant. Food wouldn't stay down, and she was dizzy more often than not. Before her conversion to Arion she'd been unable to have children. When she'd become pregnant the news had been both exciting and terrifying at the same time. No baby had been born to this new race they had become. His mate would be the first to produce. And with that knowledge had come fear. Reality had delivered the hard truth. This was no easy path.

Holly was his life. He loved her beyond belief. And he needed her. "Let's go upstairs and I'll lie down with you."

Blowing a strand of blonde hair from her eyes, she shook her head. "I'm really onto something." She shoved a slide under the microscope. "I'm close to solving the vitamin C deficiency. But," she said, "it's better than just a cure. I have a surprise for you. It's not fully tested." She opened a drawer and pulled out a dart. "It's laced with a special steroid formula Diego and I have been perfecting. It depletes vitamin C. For most people this would be a slow process but the lab tests show different results on GTECHS. Rapid metabolism makes it race through their system and weakens their healing process. In other words, if you shoot them, they are going to feel it in ways they normally wouldn't. Bullets will be more effective."

As much as Mason wanted her to rest, he realized that this was an amazing discovery. But then she was amazing. He'd known that from the moment he'd met her. "How fast will this work?"

"Well, I can't say for sure. It's only lab tested, but if I'm right, minutes. But it needs to be injected or shot into a major artery. The neck or near the heart is the best bet. I'm working on different distribution methods. Right now I have only a few loaded tranquilizer bullets."

Holly turned towards the microscope again. "No," Mason said, walking to her and reaching for her hand.

She looked up at him, a hint of impatience in her eyes. "Mason, this is important."

"So are you," he said and pulled her to her feet. His finger brushed her cheek. "I love you, Holly Heart."

She smiled. "I love you too. Now let me look at my slide." But she grabbed her stomach and a little sound slid from her lips.

"Sick again?" he asked concerned.

She nodded. He moved before she could protest and slid his hands under her legs. "Mason!" she complained. "Put me down."

"In bed," he said. "If you won't rest, I know other ways to pass the time."

A bit of laughter slid from her lips but then she moaned again. "The movement is making it worse."

They reached the elevator just as the doors slid open. Inside stood Sterling looking like he'd been dragged behind the motorcycle he loved so much, and two other people he didn't know. One of which, he assumed, was Marcella Hunter. But one was missing who should be present.

"Where's Diego?"

Sterling leaned against the elevator wall. "Acting like he's some superhero. I had to get Marcella back."

The woman reached for the door. "That would be me but I wanted to stay. I didn't want to leave him. I could have helped."

"Put me down," Holly said.

Mason ignored her and looked at the other stranger. "Crap. You're half converted." He looked at Sterling. "What the hell is going on?"

"Put me down, Mason Alexander," Holly said. "Don't you see they need medical attention?"

Marcella stepped forward and reached for Holly's hand. "So do you."

Mason looked at this newcomer, feeling a glimmer of hope. "Can you help her?"

She nodded but her eyes were big and hinted at tears. "Please go get Diego and my aunt."

Mason sighed. "I need a rundown of what's going on and fast." He stepped forward. "Everyone upstairs. Sterling needs to eat and so do you…"

"The name is David."

They all faced the front of the elevator as the doors shut. "Welcome to our world, David. It's not much of a party, but it's never boring."

* * * * *

The room was as normal as a bedroom in a typical modern-looking home. It had pictures on the walls. Decorations around the room. Even very modern-looking black finished furnishings. It was almost possible to forget they were several levels beneath the ground.

Marcella sat on the edge of the bed where Holly lay looking too pale. She reached for her hand to confirm what she already sensed. Whatever was wrong was not yet fatal. She focused…but it could be.

Sterling sat nearby in a chair, orange juice in one hand and his third sandwich in the other. He was looking better but some of his cuts were deep. "I can help you," she said to him. "I'm weak now, but if I rest I can help."

A smile filled Sterling's face. "I appreciate the offer but save your energy for people who need it." He held up the orange juice. "You saw Michael's wrist. We heal quickly as long as we have enough vitamin C and nourishment."

"And sleep," Holly added.

Sterling ignored her. "By tomorrow I'll be ready to fight again."

Holly snorted. "Hardly. The day after tomorrow. You're not a super hero, Sterling."

"That's not what she said."

Marcella blinked. "She?"

Holly made a face. "He's being a man. Ignore him. Pretending to be a ladies' man. He doesn't even want a woman right now. He has no mate."

"Back in the day the ladies did call me super." He wiggled his brows.

Marcella laughed but heavy thoughts were in her mind. She wanted to ask about this mating they all talked about. Could Diego really never want another?

Sterling answered her unasked question. "Diego is lucky to have found you, Marcella."

Holly pushed to a sitting position. "What?" She surprised Marcella by lifting her hair and touching her neck. "Oh my God! I can't believe it. You're Diego's woman. I had so hoped for his day to come."

Marcella turned to her and slid her fingers to her neck. "I…don't understand all of this."

She looked across the room, feeling the male eyes on her. Mason was taping Sterling's injuries after forcing Holly to simply supervise his actions. But his eyes were on her. David had already been given an injection of some sort and was resting in some separate cavern. She was glad he wasn't here, considering the subject now on the table.

It was all very overwhelming. Holly squeezed her arm, drawing her gaze. "We'll talk later."

And then, as if taking a cue from Holly he changed the subject. Or maybe he just wanted to move on to more critical matters. Whatever the reason, she was glad to be out of the hotspot.

"So where is Michael?" Mason asked. "When was the last time you saw him?"

"Mexico," Sterling said. "I don't know where the hell he is. We haven't seen him or Marcus since we went lights out and woke up in 51. I hope like hell they are helping Diego."

Mason finished wrapping the last open cut on Sterling. "Well, I can't take a chance he's not. We've not heard from him. I'll take some men and go after Diego."

He walked to stand in front of Marcella. She looked up at him. The man they called their leader. The man who Diego so believed in and trusted. And now he was going to save Diego. Mason stared at her. "If you have the power, I ask that you heal Holly." Though his tone was flat, she felt his emotion. He was a ball of love and fear and even pain all wrapped together. "And I will bring Diego to you."

Marcella pushed to her feet. Her hand went to his arm. "Is there any hope my aunt is alive?"

"One thing Holly has taught me...there is always hope." He paused. "I need a moment with my mate."

She nodded and Sterling pushed to his feet. Marcella followed him from the room. Moments later, she stood in the middle of a living room. Or a cave carved into the image. It even had a fireplace.

Sterling sat down on the couch and motioned for her to join him. "We need to talk, Marcella."

She swallowed but she didn't move. Standing there, her fists balled by her side suddenly, she felt very alone. Who did she trust? Any of these people? How did she know their agenda?

The man she wanted and needed might have been the very one who had caused her aunt's death. And he was the reason she was now holding weapons and ready to become murderer over healer. She didn't like what she had become.

"He told the Arions to kill me, not Catherine. They made him choose who would die first and he knew to say me. I had the most chance of living because of how my body works."

Marcella felt the words like a punch in the stomach. "What?"

"Yes," he said. "And the Arions laughed. They saw it for what it was. A way to protect Catherine and David. They would have killed all of us but you in the end. Diego might have lived. He has skills they need. But only if he changed sides and he would have died before he did that. He didn't betray you."

Marcella felt her knees tremble. Diego didn't do what she thought. She felt the heat of panic. She'd told him she hated him. And now he could die with those words in his mind.

* * * * *

Mason sat down next to Holly. "I have to go."

"I know," she said, but her lip trembled. "How many men are you taking?"

"Only a few. Unless I take an army, this is covert. A few strong men in and out."

"At least take the new steroid bullets." She squeezed his arm. "And come back."

He pulled her close and kissed her. Would this hell call war ever end?

Chapter Fourteen

🙚

Mason was indeed a strong leader. Diego often looked back at his decisions and recognized his good judgment. Like now. It had been decided months before that if ever the Knights were separated they would meet up at one of several underground checkpoints. Diego stood above ground at one of these designated areas, examining his entry points to the 51 compound debating his options. Diego knew his chances of finding Catherine alive weren't good. Damion was as ruthless as they came. He wanted power and he would do anything to get it. But he had to try to save Marcella's only living family member.

Suddenly, Michael appeared by his side. His heart about jumped out of his chest. "Shit," Diego said in a hissed whisper. "How the hell do you do that without even a flutter of wind?"

"Practice," Michael said. "Something you don't have. You spend too much time in the lab."

Marcus stepped forward and handed Diego a bag of peanuts and a bottle of orange juice. Diego eyed him and accepted what was offered. "I thought you two were dead."

"No plans to go and do that anytime soon," Michael said. "But if you were going in there alone, I'd say you had a death wish."

Diego stared at the complex and took a long, much-needed drink of orange juice. The middle of the night was the best time to make a move. He doubted anyone knew they were gone yet. And any chance of finding Catherine alive meant acting now.

"Who's still inside?" Marcus asked.

Diego took a few moments to answer, thinking about the repercussions of returning without good news. "Catherine."

Silence. Michael finally spoke. "Marcella is not handling this well, I take it."

"No." Diego didn't look at either of them.

Michael stared at the man he had grown to know and trust and realized what a turning point this was for him and his mate. He had been alone for years now and he had learned to deal with the emptiness. But inside the dark power of his beast grew stronger. It was a battle he didn't quite understand. And one he had kept silent about. He kept a distance from most. It was considered his personality. But he knew things others didn't and had powers beyond many of the other Knights. He wasn't sure why he was different but he knew Mason had dealt with a similar reality.

Holly had already voiced concerns about the GTECH enhanced men and a need to get them mated. About how it seemed to affect them if they didn't. Perhaps it was the need for a mate that burned inside him. Michael had been one of the first converted, as had Mason. His time without a mate had been the longest of all the converted males. Did this impact his stability in some mental or physical way? There was so much they still didn't know about the needs of this new race they had become. Things he intended to help his people discover. But right now, he had one focus.

He needed to help Diego and his mate come together and thrive.

"You need to rest," Michael said to Diego. "We should wait until at least midnight or beyond to move forward."

In silent agreement, the Knights found shelter in the hidden cave. They spent the next few minutes explaining what had gone down and making plans. They had two other men with them but it was decided they should stay on alert to assist an escape. It would be Michael and Diego who would go inside. Both had inside knowledge of the facility since they had once been trapped on the wrong side of the war.

And with only an hour to sleep, Diego sat down on the cavern floor and let his head fall to the rock wall. His eyes fluttered as his dreams drifted to Marcella.

* * * * *

With heavy eyes, Marcella looked down at Holly. She was asleep now. For hours, Marcella had lain with her. And healed the weakness in the center of her body. It wasn't poison that attached Holly. It was as if she was undernourished. Marcella wasn't sure she could protect her from such a thing. She had only eased the sickness.

When Diego returned... God, she hoped he did. Pushing the thought aside, she refused to be negative. He had to come back. And when he did, she needed to talk to him about what was wrong with Holly. This was a case where his skill as a doctor was stronger than her power as a healer. She couldn't drive nutrients into Holly's body. Her power drove away the poisons.

She walked towards the door she now knew led to the bathroom. And to a huge garden tub. Hard to believe so far underground, but it was a pleasant surprise. A hot bath would do her good. When Holly had offered she had more than eagerly accepted. Only she wanted to stay with her until she was sleeping. Marcella shut herself in the bathroom and made quick work of starting the water. To her surprise, she even found bubble bath. She wasn't quite sure she had ever felt so dirty. She piled her clothes at her feet, item by item.

Her foot touched the water and she sighed. It was like a rush of relief was already inching through her body. A moment later she settled into the tub, bubbles covering her body, and rested her head against the wall. She tried not to think about the world above. About how she would forever be underground. About what that would be like without Diego. Forcing her eyes shut, she curled her feet beneath her, turned sideways and allowed her head to settle on the plush cushion. In her mind, she called to him. *Diego.* Over and over in her mind she said his name. Hoping for an answer…until her mind went dark.

* * * * *

Marcella stepped out of the tub and reached for her towel. The mirror was directly across from her and she looked up as she began to dry her skin. Wondering what Diego saw when he looked at her. But what she found was him. Diego. She blinked. It couldn't be. He stood there, naked, cock hard with arousal, a perfect image of male perfection. In the back of her mind, she wanted to ask questions but her body ached with the vision he made.

Her nipples already damp from the bath tightened with arousal. And though he looked like a muscular Adonis, a sensual feast for her viewing, it was those deep, dark eyes of his that made her burn from the inside out. In them she saw passion but also emotion. Something deep, and untouchable, yet at the same time, it wrapped around her and caressed her skin. As if he touched her with his stare.

He moved towards her, and without thought, she did what felt necessary. Her hand found the proof of his arousal, fingers wrapping the width and then sliding towards the soft tip. She heard his intake of breath but he didn't look down. His hand went to the towel she held, and he tossed it aside. He moved so that he stood to the side of her. Almost behind her. She could feel his cock pressing against her hip and ass.

And she was tingling, wet and ready for him.

Water droplets clung to her shoulder and he used his palm to slowly erase the moisture. She shivered as goose bumps formed in the aftermath. His mouth moved close to her ear. "You know I would so anything to please you, don't you, *mi amor*?"

But she couldn't respond. His hand was now gliding over her skin, low on her back. Anticipation had her heart racing and her body thrumming with need. She felt his palm on her cheek and shivered. His fingers brushed the cleft, intimate as they slid downward.

Her eyes fluttered as she felt the glide of her silky arousal on his finger. And then his hand raised and came down over her cheek with a firm, possessive grip. Her breath hitched at the unexpected force. "Answer," he ordered. "Do you know? I need to know you know."

"Yes," she whispered, responding not to the command but the desperation she sensed in him. For a man of control, which she knew he was, he was raging with urgency. Hovering on the edge of some sort of explosion.

He slid his one hand around her hip and flattened it on her stomach, pulling her so her back molded to his chest and his cock slid between her legs. Long and hard, it slid against her wet core and made her burn for him. To have him inside her was the ultimate intimacy. Something he made her crave even if she didn't understand what she felt. Or the way it burned a path along her skin and made her stomach swirl with flutters of warmth.

He lowered her forward, urging her hands on to the sink top. Her eyes went to the mirror, watching them together. Naked. Touching. Pressed close. His lips brushed her ear, and his hand slid to her hip and he pulled her ass tight to his hips. His breath was warm on her neck.

Diego's eyes met hers in the mirror. She felt the contact clear to her toes. It was as if he crawled beneath her skin and became one with her. Any doubt he was a part of her was gone in that moment. And the control was not his. Nor was it hers. It was shared. For he wanted her as intensely as she did him. Together they formed this molten heat. Together they simply were united in passion and in life.

Slowly his gaze dropped, and it was as if he was touching her. Her breasts were high and nipples pebbled hard with the bittersweet ache of pleasure. His fingers moved to the tips and lightly brushed them. Sensual heat shot through her body and straight to her core. Her hands covered his and pressed his palms to her body. She arched into the touch and made a low growling noise. Animalistic and wild, it seemed to only fire her desire.

What was it about this man that made her want to yell for more?

But she didn't have to. In one slick move he pressed his cock to the center of her body and sunk deep. "Yes," she cried out. "Yes." Her head jerked backwards as the ripples of sensation inched through her body.

Marcella felt his hands slide down her body and settled on her hips. And he thrust into her. Hard. Deep. The intensity of what she felt made her eyes flutter, but she wanted to see him. Her man. The sexy, wild man who had taken her life by storm. And what a sight he was. Bare chest, muscles rippling with exertion, he looked like a warrior fighting for his life. For her. His face was etched with pleasure as he drove into her. Over and over, he hit her core in a crazed pounding that seemed to answer the pleas of her body but then leave her wanting more.

And suddenly, she couldn't keep her eyes open. A ball of tension was forming right above her clit…his cock slid along the spot with delicious friction. It danced along her nerve endings and made her moan. Her body was at that point of no return. She was tumbling but it wasn't quite there. But his hands slid around the front of her thighs and one slid to her breast. The minute he pinched her nipple she rolled into bliss.

The pleasure was so intense she actually felt her body jerk and then tremble. Long, hard spasms sent her into sensations of absolute heaven. So much so that she hardly knew when Diego joined her. It wasn't until she began to sink into the aftermath that she heard his gasp and felt his last shudder of release. And then he leaned forward as she pulled herself upward. They rested against the sink, his body tight against hers. He ran his hand down her hair, and his fingers brushed her cheek, urging her lips to his.

Long, loving strokes of his tongue swept along hers. Reluctantly, he pulled away. She felt his hesitation. "Do you know, right this moment, that I love you?"

She could barely breathe, so intense was the emotion she felt. "Yes," she whispered and dear God, she did. She really did. They'd hardly just met and she knew he loved her and she loved him.

He smiled and she realized she hadn't seen him do that much. She wanted him to do it more often. She wanted to be the reason. "Just like this very moment," he said, "you can reach me with you mind. All you have to do is believe."

* * * * *

Marcella shivered and her eyes flew open. The water around her was cold. Where...what...she sat up. Water dripped from her body. Diego. Where was he? Her eyes moved around the bathroom but he was nowhere to be found. It had been too real. Her body felt ripe with arousal. Touched. Burning with the feel of his hands.

Slowly, she sank back against the wall and pressed her eyes shut. "I love you too," she whispered. *I love you too.*

Chapter Fifteen

ഔ

They appeared at the far west side of Area 51. Two men from the wind. Above, the sky twinkled with the lights of distant planets. Of stars that held more secrets than most of humanity began to comprehend. Neither spoke. They didn't have to. Both knew what had to be done.

With the speed of knowledge and skill of hunters, they opened a hidden doorway leading to an underground facility. Already the inner radar of the Arions would be alerting the enemy of their arrival. But once underground, they would be undetectable. A ventilation system tunnel, their chosen spot held no cameras. Like ghosts, they entered a facility so secure most would find it impossible to breach. But then most were not like them. Inside it was dark but with eyes unlike a human's the blackness was no deterrent. In a few short minutes, they were at the entrance to the prison cells.

Diego stopped at a large metal casing. Beneath them two guards leaned against the walls. But their true obstacle was the camera in the corner. The one that threatened to alert the forces of many. This was where Diego had to believe in the newfound powers he and Marcella had together. He'd reached for her in her sleep for a reason. Actually, for a lot of reasons. Most importantly, in case he didn't make it home. He wanted her to know what she was to him. And he to her.

But unlike the first shared dream, he had been awake while she had slept. He had intentionally found her with his mind. The ability to do and say what he intended, to make every breath feel real, had been incredible. And afterwards, he had assured Michael he had the ability to fool that camera. Everything he had been able to do prior to mating, he could do ten times better and he hadn't even tried. It was effortless. Her unique skill had melded into his.

Diego focused on the camera, playing the scene of the two unmoving guards in his mind. Willing it to replay on the camera. But a flash of doubt played in his mind. There was so much on the line here. He thought of his mate and instinctively reached for her mind. Worried about her future and how his failure would impact her. If he was wrong...and then, like the caress of a feather, Marcella was in his head.

I am here.

Michael touched his arm, asking if they could move without words. And in that moment Diego knew the answer. He looked at his friend and gave a quick nod of his chin. They were on the ground, guards shot in the head with silent bullets in a matter of sixty seconds. Then each took a cell door. With the guards' keys they were inside in another twenty seconds. Only what Diego found was not what was expected. At least ten women lined the walls, chained by their wrists and drugged. Not one of them even moved. Few wore clothes.

He didn't take long to think. Catherine wasn't here. No way could he rescue them. Not now. They'd all die in the process. He started for the door and Michael entered. "Same thing in the next cell."

181

That left one more. Without another word they went there. And what they found was the same. Only this time he found what he came for. Catherine. His heart squeezed at the site. She was bruised and bloody and chained to the wall. And he knew without taking her pulse she was also dead.

The minute he made the discovery, he tried to block his thoughts. To protect Marcella. But it was too late. He heard her scream in his head. Felt the pain like a stab in his heart.

Nooooooo!

Marcella...

But he couldn't feel her. She had withdrawn from his mind. Gone.

Michael touched his shoulder. "We must leave."

Diego nodded and turned away from Catherine. Wishing like hell he could bring her back.

* * * * *

Marcella sat on the bathroom floor, tugging her robe tighter around her body. Tears rolled down her cheeks. It hurt. It hurt so much. And suddenly she felt the comfort of arms around her. Holly. She hugged her and pulled her close. How long she cried she didn't know. It was as if her very soul tore from her chest. She cried for her aunt. And she cried for the parents taken from her at such a young age. All her life her differences had destroyed everyone she loved.

Finally, desperate for answers, she spoke. "They...killed her," she whispered. "Why?"

Holly leaned back and used a tissue to wipe Marcella's cheek. "There is no answer to this. They are evil. It's why I work so hard to find ways to fight them."

She rejected the implications of her words. Right now, she could reject life. It felt like dying might be better than the ache inside. "I don't want to do this. I don't kill. I heal."

"I felt the same," Holly said. "I'm a doctor and a scientist. My family spent their entire lives trying to find ways to heal and cure illness. But I've accepted that my skills must be used to stop these monsters." She touched her stomach. "Though you might not believe it right now, I've learned to fight. I can shoot a gun and even handle a knife. You name it. I'm fully converted but I don't have a lot of the extras Mason has. No knifed arms or fangs. I learned to use weapons."

Marcella blinked. "What? Fangs?

Holly laughed. "You have much to learn. The bottom line tonight is, I will fight and I will kill an Arion if necessary. But even more so, I use my skills to help others fight. We must win this war."

Marcella was starting to grasp what was needed. A light was glowing inside, pressing her to go on. To help. "And I can do the same. That's what you're saying."

Holly nodded. "Yes. It's not about healing as much as it is about your other skills. Arions know how to levitate and use their minds in ways the Knights don't. Knights are the same species. This means they can do what the Arions can, they just don't know how."

Marcella understood. "But I'm not sure I can help."

"All we ask is that you try. Teach what you do naturally. You were born with your powers. Knights weren't. What you do they must learn."

It made sense. And it gave her a purpose. She so needed that right now.

As if she read her mind, Holly reached for her hand. "Diego needs you. The bond is hard to understand but it is strong." She paused. "And so very special."

Marcella stared at her. "He says I belong to him."

Holly laughed. "Men. Just make sure he knows he belongs to you as well."

And when Marcella thought it was impossible, she smiled.

Because Diego did know he belonged to her.

Chapter Sixteen

𝕤𝕺

As easily as they had appeared inside the compound, Diego and Michael reappeared on the outskirts. Marcus and two other men were to meet them at a certain checkpoint. They appeared inside the cluster of trees established as the meeting stop. And as expected Marcus was there. Only he stood in the midst of four Arions, one of which was Damion, and he wasn't a captive.

Marcus was a traitor.

"Welcome," Damion said. "Took you long enough."

Michael stepped towards him, razors extended, paying no attention to the others around them. And just like that, they were in the midst of a battle. Diego followed his lead and extended his razors. There was no time to draw weapons. He simply had to go hand to hand. With an Arion on either side of him, he felt the slice of his side as it ripped beneath a razor.

But he also sliced the face of another. He couldn't stay in one spot and survive and he knew it. With a move he normally wouldn't attempt, he disappeared into the wind and reappeared several feet away. He'd never been able to do such a thing. Michael could, as could Mason. And even in danger, his mind went to Marcella. It was the power she had blessed him. She had made this possible.

He had a moment to take stock. His eyes went to Michael as he drove one of his razors through the head of

Marcus. Sure death. At the same time, he kicked another. But Damion was missing.

His two Arions appeared beside him, and once again he was in heated battle. The punches came hard and fast but he held his own. These two, he determined, were newly converted. He was easily able to hold them off. They had yet to develop a high level of skills. And he wondered why they were chosen as his attackers.

Was the intent simply to distract him?

With his urgency on the rise, he slammed a knife through the head of one of them and turned to find the other. He needed to figure out what was really going on here. Only he now faced Damion. The other Arion was gone. He and Damion stood there, face-to-face, eyes locked in challenge. In the distance, Diego was aware that Michael was surrounded.

Damion had an agenda. "What do you want?" Diego asked.

He smiled, completely confident in his intent. "You and Marcella."

"It won't happen."

"I have a feeling your mate will come if it saves your life. After all, her aunt is gone. You are all she has."

"You bastard," Diego said, stepping forward. He was going to kill him here and now. The intent had been to kill Catherine all along. But suddenly he had three Arions around him, knives at his throat.

Damion laughed. "Rash actions will get you killed, my old friend."

"We are not friends." He should attempt to fade and move. But if he failed...

Damion continued, "Not yet but we will be." He spoke the words with confidence.

The knives were close. A wrong move and Diego would be dead. He knew he needed a miracle. And it came in the form of bullets smashing into the chests of the men around him. The moment was all he had. Diego disappeared into wind and reappeared several feet away. Seconds later, Mason appeared by his side. Knights were in hard battle, and the Arions were falling as if powerless. The steroid. It worked.

There was one Arion still standing. Damion. Knights surrounded him, ready to end this battle. "Wait!" Diego called. "He's mine."

Diego started forward but Mason reached for his arm. "No. Go to your mate. He is not worth it. This is not who you are."

The words hit him like a punch in the gut. Mason was right. He had been eager to kill. The beast inside raged with urgency. Because of Damion. Which was exactly why he needed to walk away. Michael appeared by his side and he and Diego exchanged a look. It was time to go home. They disappeared into the wind, leaving Mason and the other Knights to end this battle.

And it was indeed over for now though not even close to done. Mason wasn't surprised when his brother appeared by his side. David. The newcomer in their camp shared his name. That was going to be difficult for him. Anything that reminded him of his brother was like poison.

He turned to face the man once called family and now called enemy. But David wasn't here to fight. Mason sensed his intent.

'"Join me, Mason."

"Never."

"You can't win."

Mason's brow inched upward. "Then what are you afraid of?"

David laughed. "Perhaps it's you that is afraid. That is why you hide, isn't it?"

"I'm here now. Fight me."

"I want us to rule together, Mason. I will not kill the man who can own the universe with me. Together we can have it all. Think of it. Our resources combined. We can make a better race. No more crime. No more racism."

"And what do you call your treatment of humans?"

"Necessary. They are fools who abuse each other and their planet."

"You're the fool, David. And I'm going to stop you."

He smiled. "I haven't given up on you yet." The wind lifted around them and David's jaw clenched. "But I warn you, my patience is thin."

And then he was gone.

* * * * *

Diego followed Michael off the elevator and found Marcella at the doors. She wrapped her arms around him and clung. He had expected Holly to tell her he had arrived. They had cameras and buzzers to alert them of arrivals. But he hadn't expected this kind of greeting. He held her and buried his nose in the soft scent of her hair. Never in his life had he needed someone like he needed Marcella. She wasn't blaming him for her aunt. He had been certain that she would.

Michael slid by them in silence. He stopped in front of Holly and answered her question before she asked. "Mason is safe. He'll be here soon."

Marcella looked at her hand and then Diego's side. "You're bleeding!

Holly rushed forward. "Let me see." Her hand was on his side. "Come with me. You need stitches."

She started walking and Diego reached for her hand. "No. How are you?"

Holly smiled. "Thanks to Marcella, I'm not sick for the first time in a week."

Diego looked at Marcella, a question in his eyes.

I can't heal her. I only calmed her body. She is not getting the nutrients her body needs. You must heal her, Diego.

How serious is she? Can you buy me some time to find an answer to the absorption issues?

Marcella bit her bottom lip. *Some.*

Holly frowned. "Stop talking about me in your heads. Tell me what you're saying."

Diego sighed. "We have to solve the absorption issues."

"I have some ideas on that. Now come get stitched and well so you can help me make them count." She paused. "Tomorrow."

* * * * *

Marcella felt Diego's lips on hers and her eyes opened instantly. They were lying in the bed Diego had called theirs. It was a small cavern behind Holly and Mason's. She'd fallen asleep in his arms. And he had held her as she cried for her aunt.

Her palms went to his cheeks. "Tell me I'm not dreaming."

He smiled against her lips. "You weren't dreaming before. It was more like an alternate existence."

Her hand brushed his bandage. "What about your side?"

"I've slept several hours. It's much better." His lips brushed hers again. "You have no idea how much I need you."

"I'm beginning to," she said. "I need you too. I don't understand all of this but I do." Marcella paused. "Make me like you, Diego."

He leaned back and looked into her eyes. "What?"

"Holly said she converted."

"Or she would have died. She was injured."

"You don't want me to?" she asked, her teeth finding her bottom lip.

"I do. I mean…I don't know. You have more ability to protect yourself if you convert."

"Good. I want to fight. I want to win this war."

Diego brushed hair from her eyes. His touched made her shiver. It warmed and enticed as well as making her feel loved and needed. "You hate fighting," he said.

"So do a lot of soldiers," Marcella objected. She'd thought this through. "I would rather contribute in other ways but I won't be defenseless."

"There are negatives to conversion," he warned. "Look at Holly and this pregnancy."

"We'll solve the nutrition issues. I know we will. But if we don't take the advantages the enhancements offer, we might not live to save humanity."

Diego slid between her legs, and his elbows rested on either side of her head. "Give it time. If you want this, I want it. But not now."

Her fingers pressed on his chest. "First you pressed me to accept and now you press me to wait. I don't understand you."

"Mi hermosa," he said, the words gliding off his tongue like sweet seduction. The heat of anger was quickly turning to sizzle. "I pushed you because I had to. Now I give you the choice." He kissed her cheek, her chin and her lips. "When you choose to fully convert, I want you to really want it. To know it's right. I promised myself I would not take. What comes next you must give freely and take the time to be certain." He paused. "You choose what comes next."

Emotion tightened in her chest. And now she understood what had been all along. He didn't own her nor did she own him. They shared one another. Her hands went to his face, and her finger traced his lip. "I choose to fight. And I choose us."

Enjoy An Excerpt From
RED HOT SECRETS

Copyright © LISA RENEE JONES, 2005.

For long moments, they stared at one another, the air charged with electricity. With attraction. Then, he wasn't sure which one of them moved, maybe they both did, but suddenly, they were kissing. His lips slanted over hers, taking what he wanted with a greedy exploration of tongue against tongue. Lauren's hands did a slow slide up his arms, until her hands joined behind his neck.

Sinking into the kiss, he felt her melt, inch by inch, until her breast pressed against his chest. With a low growl, Matt merged with her, hip to hip, molding her softness to his hardness. The fire she evoked was like nothing he'd ever known. It simply wasn't possible to get close enough. Lifting her leg to his waist, his hand flattened on her thigh and slid her skirt upward. At the same time, he centered his cock into the V of her body, wishing for no barriers. Ready to strip her naked and drive deep into the silky recesses of her body.

In the back of his mind, the voice of reason called to him. He didn't want this to end. Slow down. He had to slow down. To savor and relish. Yet, each moment drove him closer to the edge. Hell, he'd not even managed to get her out of her clothes. He damn sure wanted to enjoy that part of this night.

As if she wanted to test his resolve, Lauren's hands slid down Matt's back leaving a trail of heat where she touched. When her palms flattened on his thighs, fingers near his pulsing sex, he barely resisted the urge to seize her hand and move it to his cock.

Taking a deep breath, he forced himself to hold back. Lauren was a bit timid and he didn't want to scare her. He wanted to let her do this at her own pace. Something told him Lauren needed that freedom. For once, it might be nice to let someone else drive. It was an interesting thought. One that deserved consideration. Yet, deep down he knew he was a man who took what he wanted. He valued control and his enjoyment came with more intensity when he had it under thumb. Still, with Lauren, he found himself considering...willing to see where this would go.

Lauren took the lead but her exploration was tentative. He could tell she held back her passion. As if she didn't know what to do with the power he had silently handed over. A series of gentle caresses. A touch here. A touch there. When she tugged at his shirt, and lifted her eyes his, he saw the silent plea in her gaze. And then it hit him. She wasn't ready for control. Lauren wanted it but she didn't know how to take it.

He needed to push her over the edge and then hand her back the key.

Momentarily, he let her leg ease to the floor. Matt stepped backwards and reached for the front of his shirt, considering the best method of bringing Lauren out of her shell. He couldn't believe how much he wanted to pull her close again. His body raged angrily at the loss of contact. Yet, at the same time, he enjoyed the building tension. He could feel the rise of the heat. The burn that signaled an upcoming explosion. And he knew it would be well worth the wait.

He fingered his buttons, and Lauren watched each one as he touched it. Amazingly, just knowing how attentive she was pushed his urgency an extra degree higher. Somehow, he managed to take his time, wanting the flame he saw in her eyes to turn to a fire.

The air, thick with desire, seemed to enclose them, as if it circled their bodies, and drew them together.

The instant he completed his task, Matt leaned forward and pressed his palms on either side of her head. "Take your clothes off," he said, his voice low and powerful.

Why an electronic book?

We live in the Information Age—an exciting time in the history of human civilization, in which technology rules supreme and continues to progress in leaps and bounds every minute of every day. For a multitude of reasons, more and more avid literary fans are opting to purchase e-books instead of paper books. The question from those not yet initiated into the world of electronic reading is simply: *Why?*

1. *Price.* An electronic title at Ellora's Cave Publishing and Cerridwen Press runs anywhere from 40% to 75% less than the cover price of the exact same title in paperback format. Why? Basic mathematics and cost. It is less expensive to publish an e-book (no paper and printing, no warehousing and shipping) than it is to publish a paperback, so the savings are passed along to the consumer.

2. *Space.* Running out of room in your house for your books? That is one worry you will never have with electronic books. For a low one-time c ost, you can purchase a handheld device specifically designed for e-reading. Many e-readers have large, convenient screens for viewing. Better yet, hundreds of titles can be stored within your new library—on a single microchip. There are a variety of e-readers from different manufacturers. You can also read e-books on your PC or laptop computer. (Please note that Ellora's

Cave does not endorse any specific brands. You can check our websites at www.ellorascave.com or www.cerridwenpress.com for information we make available to new consumers.)

3. *Mobility*. Because your new e-library consists of only a microchip within a small, easily transportable e-reader, your entire cache of books can be taken with you wherever you go.

4. *Personal Viewing Preferences.* Are the words you are currently reading too small? Too large? Too… ANNOYING? Paperback books cannot be modified according to personal preferences, but e-books can.

5. *Instant Gratification.* Is it the middle of the night and all the bookstores near you are closed? Are you tired of waiting days, sometimes weeks, for bookstores to ship the novels you bought? Ellora's Cave Publishing sells instantaneous downloads twenty-four hours a day, seven days a week, every day of the year. Our webstore is never closed. Our e-book delivery system is 100% automated, meaning your order is filled as soon as you pay for it.

Those are a few of the top reasons why electronic books are replacing paperbacks for many avid readers.

As always, Ellora's Cave and Cerridwen Press welcome your questions and comments. We invite you to email us at Comments@ellorascave.com or write to us directly at Ellora's Cave Publishing Inc., 1056 Home Avenue, Akron, OH 44310-3502.

THE
☥ ELLORA'S CAVE ☥
LIBRARY

Stay up to date with Ellora's Cave Titles in
Print with our Quarterly Catalog.

Now Available!

Ellora's Cavemen
Dreams of the Oasis I

A special edition anthology of six
sizzling stories from Ellora's Cave's
Mistresses of Romantica.
Edited by Raelene Gorlinsky

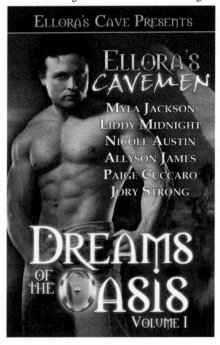

Featuring:

**Myla Jackson, Liddy Midnight, Nicole Austin,
Allyson James, Paige Cuccaro, Jory Strong**

Call Me Barbarian By Liddy Midnight

Princess Cedilla enjoys unprecedented privilege in a society where women are neither seen nor heard. Her life changes when twin barbarian gladiators enter the arena. One glance and Cedilla is irrevocably bound to these Southern warriors — and revealed as half-barbarian herself. Whether in the arena or the bedchamber, Asterix and Apostroph live for the moment — until they find their destined mate. When Cedilla is banished by the Emperor, they devote themselves to satisfying her wildest desires. But the Empire needs Cedilla, and the Empire is intolerant of barbarians...

Dragonmagic By Allyson James

It's hell to be a dragon enslaved. Arys, a powerful silver dragon in human form, is bound to a witch who uses his magic and his body to pleasure her in every way imaginable. When Arys spies Naida, a young woman just coming into her powers, watching Arys performing erotic acts with the witch, he knows that Naida is the key to his freedom. First he must convince Naida she's his true mate and that the power of their sexual play, and her love, will release him.

Fallen For You By Paige Cuccaro

For ten thousand years, Zade's warrior mentality kept him focused on the Watcher's mission — rid the world of the Oscurità fallen angels. And then the witch Isabel came under his care. The Oscurità will be coming to posses her or kill her, drawn by her burgeoning powers. Isabel is a temptation they can't ignore, but neither can Zade. If he succumbs to his feelings, Zade's frozen soul could destroy Isabel. If he resists, his unsatisfied need may cost him everything. To save all he holds dear, Zade must trust that Isabel was born for him, and he has fallen for her.

Spontaneous Combustion By Nicole Austin

Dr. Madailein Flannagan's carnal desires are blazing deep inside, and her best friend Jake Cruise is just the man to fan the flames. But the sexy, bad boy firefighter goes for equally bad girls, and Maddy's afraid she's just not his type. Although lately she has been fantasizing about Jake and a few of his friends... Jake thinks that Maddy is way out of his league, but he knows that she can't refuse a challenge. And he's come up with an irresistible dare guaranteed to send her body up in flames, gain her submission, and maybe even win her heart.

The Ambassador's Widow By Myla Jackson

Chameleon Agent Andre Batello is sent on assignment to "fill in" for an ambassador who died the night before a long-negotiated peace treaty is due to be signed. As part of a special team of individuals with the ability to assume another's identity based on a single strand of DNA, Andre's mission is to infiltrate the ambassador's life and sign that treaty. The one major glitch in his mission: he didn't plan on falling in love with the ambassador's widow.

The Joining By Jory Strong

On the water world of Qumaar, Siria Chaton is a prisoner of her talent. With her credits dwindling, she has few options and little hope for a future. Until Jett and Mozaiic du'Zehren enter her life.

After five years of being a couple, Jett and Mozaiic have gained permission to add a third, a woman, to their joining. They can't believe their good fortune when the woman assigned to them is a water diviner. Now if only she'll accept them as lovers and come home with them to the forbidden desert planet of Adjara.

MAKE EACH DAY MORE *EXCITING* WITH OUR

ELLORA'S CAVEMEN

CALENDAR

www.EllorasCave.com

COMING TO A BOOKSTORE NEAR YOU!

ELLORA'S CAVE

Bestselling Authors Tour

erridwen, the Celtic Goddess of wisdom, was the muse who brought inspiration to storytellers and those in the creative arts. Cerridwen Press encompasses the best and most innovative stories in all genres of today's fiction. Visit our site and discover the newest titles by talented authors who still get inspired - much like the ancient storytellers did, once upon a time.

Cerridwen Press
www.cerridwenpress.com

Discover for yourself why readers can't get enough of
the multiple award-winning publisher

Ellora's Cave.

Whether you prefer e-books or paperbacks,

be sure to visit EC on the web at
www.ellorascave.com

for an erotic reading experience that will leave you
breathless.